"I promise I'll keep you safe until we figure this out. I swear I won't let anyone hurt you."

"And my baby," she demanded, her voice trembling. "Will you protect my baby, as well?"

"With my life."

She knew he meant what he said. Max would not give his word lightly. She had learned that about him four months ago. He'd sworn to protect her and her child. She had to trust that. They were still on shaky ground on some levels and things were far too complicated for her to tell him the truth about the baby just yet, but they were making progress. For that, she was immensely relieved. For the first time in her adult life she admitted to herself that she truly needed someone.

And right now, that someone was Max.

Dear Harlequin Intrigue Reader,

Beginning this October, Harlequin Intrigue has expanded its lineup to *six* books! Publishing two more titles each month enables us to bring you an extraordinary selection of breathtaking stories of romantic suspense filled with exciting editorial variety—and we encourage you to try all that we have to offer.

Stock up on catnip! Caroline Burnes brings back your favorite feline sleuth to beckon you into a new mystery in the popular series FEAR FAMILIAR. This four-legged detective sticks his whiskers into the mix to help clear a stunning stuntwoman's name in *Familiar Double*. Up next is Dani Sinclair's new HEARTSKEEP trilogy starting with *The Firstborn*—a darkly sensual gothic romance that revolves around a sinister suspense plot. To lighten things up, bestselling Harlequin American Romance author Judy Christenberry crosses her beloved BRIDES FOR BROTHERS series into Harlequin Intrigue with *Randall Renegade*—a riveting reunion romance that will keep you on the edge of your seat.

Keeping Baby Safe by Debra Webb could either passionately reunite a duty-bound COLBY AGENCY operative and his onetime lover—or tear them apart forever. Don't miss the continuation of this action-packed series. Then Amy J. Fetzer launches our BACHELORS AT LARGE promotion featuring fearless men in blue with *Under His Protection*. Finally, watch for *Dr. Bodyguard* by debut author Jessica Andersen. Will a hunky doctor help penetrate the emotional walls around a lady genius before a madman closes in?

Pick up all six for a complete reading experience you won't forget!

Enjoy,

Denise O'Sullivan
Senior Editor
Harlequin Intrigue

KEEPING BABY SAFE

DEBRA WEBB

HARLEQUIN®

TORONTO • NEW YORK • LONDON
AMSTERDAM • PARIS • SYDNEY • HAMBURG
STOCKHOLM • ATHENS • TOKYO • MILAN • MADRID
PRAGUE • WARSAW • BUDAPEST • AUCKLAND

ISBN 0-373-22732-9

KEEPING BABY SAFE

Visit us at www.eHarlequin.com

Printed in U.S.A.

ABOUT THE AUTHOR

Debra Webb was born in Scottsboro, Alabama, to parents who taught her that anything is possible if you want it badly enough. She began writing at age nine. Eventually she met and married the man of her dreams, and tried some other occupations, including selling vacuum cleaners and working in a factory, a day-care center, a hospital and a department store. When her husband joined the military, they moved to Berlin, Germany, and Debra became a secretary in the commanding general's office. By 1985 they were back in the States, and finally moved to Tennessee, to a small town where everyone knows everyone else. With the support of her husband and two beautiful daughters, Debra took up writing again, looking to mysteries and movies for inspiration. In 1998 her dream of writing for Harlequin came true. You can write to Debra with your comments at P.O. Box 64, Huntland, Tennessee 37345.

Books by Debra Webb

HARLEQUIN INTRIGUE

HARLEQUIN AMERICAN ROMANCE

*Colby Agency
**The Specialists

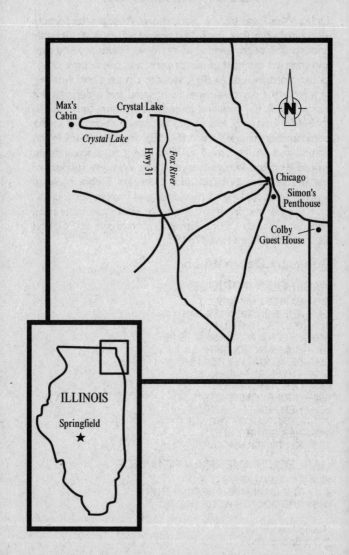

CAST OF CHARACTERS

Pierce Maxwell, "Max"—One of the Colby Agency's finest investigators. Former DEA, he will stop at nothing to protect the woman who stole his heart in a South American jungle.

Olivia Jackson, "Scout"—A private investigator and recovery agent.

Douglas Cooper—Douglas is new to the Colby Agency. He has left his Martha's Vineyard roots behind and is in search of a career that will fulfill him.

Simon Ruhl—One of Victoria Colby's most treasured finds. Formerly with the FBI, the enigmatic Simon Ruhl is a valuable asset to the agency.

Regis Brandon—CEO of Alexon, a major research corporation. Brandon is determined to undo the damage done by his predecessor. But he's hiding something…. Only time will tell if he is friend or foe.

Harold Arnold—Head of security at Alexon. Though not related by blood, Scout has thought of Harold as an uncle her entire life.

Gage Kimble—Gage served under Scout's father in Special Forces. After her father's death, he and Scout had a brief affair that evolved into an engagement. But can she trust him?

There is nothing more tragic than losing a child, whether that child has been born or still sleeps deep in a mother's womb. This book is dedicated to Dakota Jeffrey, the grandchild I will never hold in my arms but who will always live in my heart.

Prologue

In one fluid movement, Victoria Colby scooted onto
the long vanity counter's smooth marble top. "Make
yourself comfortable, Max," she insisted, with a
wave of her hand toward the small sitting area.

Pierce Maxwell surveyed the sleek decor of the
ladies' room and knew without question that getting
comfortable would be virtually impossible. "I'll
stand, thank you," he said politely, his smile equally
courteous, since he didn't want to tick off the boss.

He and Victoria were meeting in the ladies' room
because the rest of the fourth floor that housed the
Colby Agency was currently standing in about three
inches of water. The sprinkler system had gone hay-
wire and flooded the place. Plumbers and cleanup
personnel were scrambling to undo the damage
pronto. Since the tiled bathroom floors were
equipped with drains, the men's and ladies' rooms
were the only ones not requiring wading boots at the
moment. Thus the expansive ladies' room now
served as the boss's office and briefing room. Certainly no one would expect Victoria Colby to con-
duct business in the men's room.

"I have a case that I believe requires your partic-

ular expertise,'' Victoria began as she picked up a
soggy manila folder and opened it to scan the mea-
ger contents. ''As I recall, you spent a good deal of
time in South America while involved with the
DEA.''

Max nodded. ''Three long years.'' What most
didn't know was that, while with the Drug Enforce-
ment Agency, he had spent the vast majority of his
time chasing leads from informants in those hot,
steamy jungles. Max had been part of a special covert operations team that set up housekeeping in Colombia to facilitate the reduction in the flow of drugs
onto American soil. When politics, American as
well as Colombian, put an end to his team's operations, Max had grown disgusted with the bureau-
cracy and walked away. The Colby Agency had re-
cruited him practically before the ink dried on his
resignation papers.

''What's the situation?'' he asked, his interest definitely piqued.

''An old acquaintance of mine, Harold Atkins,
used to run a small private investigations firm down
in Houston,'' Victoria explained. ''He retired from
the business a few years ago and took a more cushy
job as head of security at Alexon.''

Max was familiar with Alexon and its reputation.
The corporation operated one of the foremost medical and biological research facilities in the country,
right here in Chicago. They played the high stakes
in a number of different arenas, from the latest in
stem cell research to biological weaponry for defense purposes. Head of security for that kind of
company would definitely be a ''cushy'' job, as Victoria put it.

Frowning thoughtfully, she closed the folder and continued, "According to Harold, Alexon set up a secret lab in the mountains near Bogotá a couple years back to work on a high-priority military project. Obviously, they needed complete secrecy. Two weeks ago the lab was destroyed and the scientist heading the project was almost captured."

Max lifted an eyebrow skeptically. "Almost?" he queried. He couldn't imagine a scientist having the know-how to elude a band of Colombian rebels. Hell, he was a highly trained agent and he'd barely escaped with his life a time or two. The alternative, a team commissioned by a rival research company, would certainly be just as ruthless and difficult to evade.

"Apparently Alexon put a lot of thought into the safety of their lead scientist and designed a sort of hidden panic room for just this kind of situation."

Now things were getting really interesting. "They need someone to go in, rescue him from his hiding place and bring him out, is that it?" Though Max wasn't fond of the place, he knew his way around the country well enough to feel completely comfortable with that kind of assignment.

Victoria sighed and seemed to consider her words for a time before going on. "Harold has already sent in a recovery agent to do the retrieval, but something went wrong."

Right, Max mused. Good old Harold just hadn't picked the right man for the job. A good deal more than mere skill was involved. An intimate knowledge of the country was required. "So now we have two guys to rescue."

"One man and one woman," Victoria corrected.

"Dr. Samuel Kirstenof is the scientist and Olivia Jackson is the woman Harold hired to retrieve him."

"Where are they now?" Things had just gone from interesting to troubling. Trying to get a helpless scientist out of the country undetected would be problematic enough. But having a woman tagging along—one who likely wouldn't appreciate having to be rescued in the first place—would only make bad matters worse.

Victoria passed the folder to Max. "You'll find all the pertinent information in here. Harold included the grid coordinates for the location from which he received the last transmission, two days ago."

Max sifted through the contents of the folder. Olivia Jackson was only twenty-two years old. He shook his head. No wonder she'd gotten herself trapped down there. She was barely old enough to drive, much less carry a weapon and elude militant rebels. What was Atkins thinking, sending a young woman like her to do an experienced man's job?

"Harold calls her Scout," Victoria said, drawing Max from his worrisome thoughts.

"Scout?" Max noted there was no photograph of Olivia Jackson, but there was a copy of Kirstenof's personnel badge. He looked to be about fifty, short and thin, with more hair on his chin than on his head.

"Olivia apparently prefers the nickname." Victoria eased off the counter and smoothed her neatly tailored suit with one hand. "Harold spoke highly of her, thinks of her as a daughter. He wanted me to relay how frightened he is for her welfare under current circumstances. And, of course, Alexon wants their scientist back unharmed."

Max's gaze met Victoria's. "Apparently," she added, her tone turning grave, "there has been a little war going on between Alexon and one of their competitors to come up with a certain new antidote the military needs. This could turn even nastier if that competitor is somehow involved."

Max shrugged mentally. Nasty competition he could deal with; it was *Scout* Jackson that concerned him. She wouldn't like him coming in to do what she hadn't been able to. That he was a man probably wouldn't help.

He closed the folder and gave Victoria a reassuring smile. "I'm on it. I'll take good care of the doc and the lady."

Victoria nodded once in acknowledgment. "Keep me informed of your progress. Doug will be providing backup for you."

Max resisted the urge to groan. Doug Cooper was the new guy at the Colby Agency. He was good, Max was certain; Victoria employed only the very best. But Doug was a rich kid who'd recently left his Martha's Vineyard roots and his Wall Street office behind to get a real job. Max liked him but wasn't sure he trusted his motives. Had he simply gotten bored with his daddy's yacht and his highbrow friends?

That was unfair and Max knew it. Doug was a nice guy. Time would tell about his motives. Judging prematurely was wrong. Max had to give his colleague a chance, just as Victoria had. She obviously had legitimate reasons for hiring him.

"Sounds good," Max told her, keeping his smile in place. "I'll bring him up to speed and then be on my way."

When he reached the door, Victoria's next words stopped him in his tracks.

"Be careful out there, Max," she said somberly. "The Colombian government is particularly restless right now. I don't want this agency to be responsible for an international incident, but more important, I don't want to lose you."

Max's smile hitched all the way to a grin this time. "Don't sweat it, Victoria. I know the place like the back of my hand. I'll be in and out of there before they even suspect I'm coming."

Chapter One

The click of a weapon easing into cocked mode echoed at the same time a cold steel barrel bored into the back of his skull.

Max froze.

Sweat trickled down his forehead; the bandanna he wore was already soaked through.

"Don't move."

Female.

American.

Could this be Olivia Jackson? Max wondered as the woman reached beneath his unbuttoned shirt to remove his weapon from his shoulder holster. He sure as hell hoped so. He'd been following the almost imperceptible trail she'd left for two days now. If he hadn't been a skilled tracker in this kind of environment he would have had no chance in hell of even getting close. She was good. Damn good. He'd allowed her to sneak up on him now to speed up the process and leave her with her pride intact. Having him show up and take over wasn't going to sit well with her.

"Are you Olivia Jackson?" he asked, as nonchalantly as possible with her disarming him. Despite the knowledge that they were on the same team, he didn't like being at a disadvantage.

"Who's asking?"

"I'm—" The unexpected feel of her hands moving down the length of his legs momentarily derailed his train of thought. She didn't plan to take any chances. He gritted his teeth when she discovered and confiscated the backup piece in his ankle holster. "—Pierce Maxwell," he growled in answer to her question.

She stood, moved in close behind him and said, "Well, Pierce Maxwell, looks like you've got a bit of a problem. This is definitely not the kind of place a guy wants to be when he's unarmed." She backed up a step. "You can turn around now."

Max clenched his jaw. He'd climbed, crawled and hacked his way through this hot, steamy jungle for two days now. Not to mention lived in this hellhole for three years not so long ago. He should just tell her that though she was good, she wasn't *that* good. The idea that she was enjoying this sent outrage rushing through his veins. But the last thing he needed was her on the defensive. Slowly he turned to face his captor.

He opened his mouth to demand to see some ID, but no words came out. His gaze riveted to long, silky black hair and clear gray eyes. The young woman staring back at him with her own expression of surprise looked as sexy as she appeared capable. This was definitely not the type he'd expected to find in the middle of a South American jungle.

"Who sent you?" she demanded, leveling her nine-millimeter in perfect alignment with his forehead.

It wasn't until then that he noticed the man cowering behind her. Short, thin, shiny bald pate, gray scraggly beard and clutching a black leather satchel to his chest…it was Kirstenof. Max needed no further ID.

"Harold Atkins sent me," he said brusquely. "He got worried when you didn't appear able to get Doc here—" he nodded toward the man beyond her "—back to American soil in a timely manner. I'm supposed to take the two of you home." He almost bit his tongue. Now he'd done it! Testosterone had obviously overridden his ability to maintain diplomacy.

The same outrage he'd felt moments ago now glinted in the steel-gray eyes glaring back at him. "Well, you're certainly off to a good start. And since no one but my uncle knows I'm here, I'm gonna trust you." She offered him his weapon and smiled, but the lovely face held no amusement. "What makes you think you can get us out of here when I haven't been able to?" The challenge in her tone was clear.

Max accepted his nine-millimeter, tucking it back into his shoulder holster. He'd already stepped in it; might as well follow through. "Lady, you'd be surprised at what I can do."

She gave him his .38 then, which he quickly slipped back into his ankle holster. "I suppose we'll see about that," she mused dryly. She shifted slightly so that the doc was in full view. "This is Dr. Samuel Kirstenof," she said. "His safety is top priority. We have to get him back home in one piece."

"Glad to see you're all right, sir," Max said by way of a greeting.

"I wouldn't be if Scout hadn't rescued me," he said, smiling weakly at the frustrating woman. "She arrived just in time. Another twenty-four hours and I would have been a goner for sure."

A frown worked its way across Max's forehead. The doc didn't look so good. In fact, he looked like hell—ghostly pale, with heavy dark circles beneath his eyes. The thick lenses of his glasses only magnified the frailty.

Max turned to the woman. "Surely you had a backup plan or, at the very least, a secondary egress route?"

She rolled her eyes impatiently. "Of course I did. When we tried to leave, both routes were covered. Someone sold me out," she said tightly. "No one knew the details of my plans except my uncle Harold and a few members of his staff. It had to be someone close to him." Her gaze narrowed as if she might just suspect him. "On second thought maybe I shouldn't trust you."

Max shrugged noncommittally. "That's something you'll have to take up with your uncle when you get back." He swiped the sweat from his brow with his shirtsleeve. "Now, if you'll just follow me, I'll get us out of here."

He ignored her muttered curses—adjectives not found in the dictionary, which she used to describe him on a very personal level—as he started to retrace his steps down the trail he'd hacked through the dense foliage. He imagined that desperation was the real reason she agreed to follow him. A grin tugged at the corners of his mouth. At least she had a sense of humor.

"Where the hell are you going?" she snapped after only a couple of minutes of moving swiftly to keep up with him. "I promise you this is definitely not the way you want to go. There's a rebel camp just—"

He turned back to her. She stumbled in an effort to stop, but only succeeded in barreling into his chest. He steadied her, the feel of her skin beneath his fingers startling him. He released her as suddenly as he'd grabbed her, and blinked repeatedly to somehow dispel or deny the confusing sensations.

"Trust me," he said, irritated at himself all over again. "I know what I'm doing."

"Famous last words," she countered as she fell back into step behind him.

The next time Max glanced over his shoulder he noted that she'd placed the doc behind him and was now bringing up the rear. A good move, he decided. The doc would be more secure that way.

Max railed silently at himself all the way down the mountain. What the hell had gotten into him? The moment he'd laid eyes on Scout Jackson he'd lost his balance. So she wasn't what he'd expected. That wasn't any reason to loose his perspective. It wasn't like he didn't have his share of female company. So why the hell was he feeling as if he were trapped on a deserted island and she was his only hope for female companionship? He shook his head. He couldn't answer that question. The heat, maybe? Whatever the cause, there was definitely something about her that spoke to him, even when she wasn't talking. She was fairly tall, and from what he could tell had a nice, athletic figure beneath her baggy attire. But it was more than that. There was some kind of chemistry going on here.

And he definitely had to get a grip. One wrong step in this country and they could all end up dead.

SCOUT HAD TO HAND IT TO Mr. Pierce Maxwell. He'd gotten them down the mountain, but that wasn't such an incredible feat. The big deal was the way he'd led them around no less than three rebel camps between them and the route to freedom. Now that had taken some doing. She would never have taken the risk.

As flustered as she was at having to admit to needing help, his skill made the admission a little easier. She'd studied him as he moved. He was more than simply good, he was one with his environment. He had to have spent some time here. He meshed with the jungle too easily, knew all the places to avoid as well as those to utilize fully. Knew how to use the lush landscape to his advantage. The only slip he'd made was in allowing her to sneak up on him. She'd even wondered if he'd allowed that to happen just to put them on somewhat of an equal footing. He'd come here knowing he was going to usurp her control of the situation—not that she'd been in control, after all—and maybe he'd let her sneak up on him so she'd feel better about it. Then again, maybe not.

She watched his fluid movements, unable to stem her growing admiration for his predatory skills. The fact that he was extremely well built and damn good-looking in a rugged sort of way only added insult to injury. He definitely had a great body.

Broad shoulders, muscled arms, lean waist and narrow hips. God, and those long legs. She'd suffered a heart palpitation or two as she'd patted him down. The face wasn't perfect, of course—a little rough, with sharp angles and firm lines, but not bad in any sense of the word. The blue eyes were an asset. Coupled with the sandy-blond hair, they made him look a little like a California surfer, only stronger and far more dangerous.

Scout shivered, then frowned. She couldn't remember the last time she'd met a guy who rattled her so. There was something about his voice—deep, rich, laced with just enough lethal charm to let you know who was boss.

And she hated it.

She absolutely hated being at the mercy of a guy like that. Why was it that women couldn't resist men like him? The strong, silent hero come to the rescue. The hunk who was ninety percent eye candy and ten percent solid, rugged rock. She'd worked so hard to be tougher than that—not to allow silly, adolescent urges to own her.

All for nothing.

Here she was, trudging through a jungle with danger all around her, and all she could do was lust after the guy.

Pathetic…truly pathetic.

The sound of footsteps behind her drew her up short. Scout halted and listened intently. Maxwell froze as well, turning slightly and stopping Kirstenof with an uplifted hand. The sound hadn't come from any of them because they were all being particularly careful to be absolutely silent. No, the sound—

An arm went around her neck and the barrel of a

weapon plowed into her temple as someone dragged her back several steps.

"*¡Detenganse! ¡No se muevan!*"

Scout swore. A rebel, judging by the sleeve of his threadbare uniform.

Maxwell remained stone still, then slowly raised his hands above his head. Dr. Kirstenof did the same.

Scout wanted to kick herself for not paying better attention. She should have heard this guy sooner. He'd probably been following them since they'd slipped past the last camp.

Slowly, very slowly, Maxwell turned the rest of the way around. Kirstenof didn't budge; he obviously took better heed of the order not to move than Maxwell did. Scout figured he didn't want to waste the time it would take to play this guy's game. Which meant she was in serious trouble here. She considered the cold steel currently jammed against her temple. If Maxwell made the wrong move she could end up dead.

She didn't like dead. Which, in her opinion, meant she had to do something before the hero got her killed. The rebel currently shaking in his boots right behind her no doubt had his own hopes of becoming a hero.

Maxwell took a step in their direction.

Scout's heart practically stopped. She didn't know him well enough to trust him this much.

"*¡No se muevan!*" the rebel shouted. His arm tightened around her neck. The smell of his sweat filled her nostrils.

Despite the command not to move, Maxwell just kept coming, one unhurried step at a time.

What the hell was he doing?

And then she knew.

The only reason this guy hadn't killed her already was that he was waiting for his backup. These guys weren't stupid. They knew a scientist would be worth big money—even if they didn't know why. The rebel needed her as a bargaining chip to get Kirstenof, so he probably wouldn't kill her unless Maxwell forced his hand. She glared at the man still coming closer. Damn, he appeared hell-bent on doing just that.

"*¡La mataré!*"

Scout swore silently again. Max ignored the guy's threat that he would kill her.

Considering she was probably about to die, she wondered briefly if God would forgive her for not attending church regularly since she was fifteen. Or for allowing Jimmy Wayne Brown to take her virginity at age sixteen. She'd tried really hard to do better since. She never drove while under the influence of alcohol. She'd never done drugs. She practiced safe sex—well, not that she'd had sex since she broke up with her fiancé. Now there was a subject she had no intention of pursuing. Especially right now. She still hadn't been to church, but she did pray occasionally. In fact, she probably needed to do that right now.

Scout closed her eyes and started reciting her favorite prayer aloud. If she was going to die, she might as well go down doing something right.

"*¿Qué hace?*" As the nervous rebel demanded to know what she was doing, he tightened his grip on her. When that didn't slow her chanting, he ordered her to stop. "*¡Pare!*"

Scout kept praying. She cracked one eye open just enough to see that Maxwell was now only a few steps away.

"Put the gun down, amigo," he said quietly, his hands still held high.

"*¡Detenganse! ¡La mato!*"

Apparently uncertain where to keep his aim, her captor loosened his grip for one instant. Scout reacted instantly, jamming her elbow into his side. The weapon in his hand went off, the bullet missing the top of her head by about two inches. She whipped around and landed a kick to his rib cage, hard enough to knock the wind out of him. Maxwell took him down from there.

"Run!" Max shouted over his shoulder. "Get the doc out of here!"

Scout didn't question his order. She knew as well as he did that the gunfire would bring the rebel's pals swooping down on them.

She hooked her arm in Kirstenof's and ran like hell, practically dragging the old man. The jungle understory wasn't as dense and impenetrable here. They could move more quickly here, except there was far less cover.

Gunfire erupted behind them. Her breath caught at the sound, but she kept going. She prayed, really prayed this time, that Maxwell would be okay. Her first priority had to be Kirstenof. That was her mission—to get him back to the good old U.S. of A. safely.

She couldn't help one final backward glance as she pushed onward. But, of course, she could see nothing.

More gunfire.

Much farther off and to the west this time.

Maxwell was leading them away from her and Kirstenof.

Tears stung her eyes as she pushed forward.

She scarcely knew the man, yet he was willing to give his life for hers and the scientist she was dragging away from danger.

Damn.

Pierce Maxwell was a hero.

Why hadn't she been nicer to him? Instead she'd let her pride get in the way and she'd resented his interference. Interference that was now saving her hide. Not to mention she hadn't fully trusted him.

Scout blinked back the moisture pooling behind her lashes as she moved steadily forward. All she had to do was get to Bogotá and she would be home free. Everything was set from there—a hotel room that only she knew about and an SUV rented under an assumed name.

Unable to help herself, she looked back yet again but there was no sign of Pierce Maxwell. There were no more gunshots. He was probably dead already, or maybe they would keep him alive long enough to torture some answers out of him. But he knew nothing about where she was going. No one, not even Harold, had known about the hotel room and SUV. But that wouldn't keep those overambitious rebels from trying to get the information out of Maxwell.

Fury welled inside Scout. How the hell could she leave him like this?

She couldn't.

As soon as she got Kirstenof to safety, she would come back for Max.

IT WAS ALMOST DARK when Scout left Kirstenof alone in the hotel room. She'd given him strict orders not to answer the door or step outside for any reason. He wasn't even supposed to peek through a window. They should be on the road by now, but she had to see if there was anything she could do to help Maxwell. She would never be able to sleep again in this lifetime if she didn't.

Kirstenof knew the location of the vehicle, and she'd left him orders to leave the hotel at midnight if she had not returned. He didn't want to do it, but he'd finally promised to follow her instructions. He was to use the cellular phone in the SUV to call in and report that he was headed out of Colombia. Help would meet him en route. That was the plan.

Scout had considered arranging air travel out of the country, but the timing was too uncontrollable to make it work. Besides, the faction after Kirstenof and whatever he carried would be expecting them to try and fly out. Ground transportation was the best bet, all things considered.

She slipped through the dark alleys until she'd made her way out of the city, then disappeared into the woods at approximately the same point from which she and Kirstenof had emerged less than one hour ago.

The darkness added another layer of apprehension to her already acute tension. But she didn't have time to waste. Fortunately, the moon was fairly bright and offered enough illumination for her to make her way through the lush foliage without being seen.

It would take her a couple of hours to reach the

spot where they had encountered resistance. After that, she would simply—

From out of the darkness a strong hand clamped around her arm. A second one closed over her mouth when she would have screamed.

"It's me," a male voice whispered harshly in her ear.

Her heart slammed hard against her rib cage as recognition flared.

Pierce Maxwell.

She whipped around in his arms and squinted in an attempt to make him out more clearly in the darkness. "Are you all right?"

"Yeah. It just took me a while to lose them. Where's the doc?"

"He's okay. Come on." She grabbed Maxwell's hand. "I'll take you to him. They're already looking for us in the city. We have to get out of here."

"You got that right," Maxwell muttered.

It wasn't until she had closed the door behind them in the hotel room that she got a good look at Maxwell. His left forearm was bleeding.

"You're hit." She moved closer, reaching out to check what was most likely a gunshot wound. "Let me—"

"No time," he argued. "We need to get out of here before we run into any more stumbling blocks."

Reluctantly, she nodded. He was right. They'd lost enough time already. The rebels methodically combing the city would reach this particular hotel eventually. "All right, but as soon as we've put some miles behind us, we should get that looked at."

He waved her off in typical male fashion. "It's nothing."

There was too much blood for it to be nothing, but Scout didn't argue. Instead, she helped Kirstenof to his feet, noting how unhealthy he, too, looked.

"Are you all right, Dr. Kirstenof?"

He nodded. "Just tired." He clutched his satchel to his chest. "I just want to get this documentation back to Alexon."

Scout produced a smile for the weary-looking old man. "I understand, sir. Let's get going then."

WITH MAX INJURED, Scout insisted on driving. He looked a little dubious, but finally relented.

Without stopping once, she drove all night and well into the next day. She'd secured all the necessary papers ahead of time. No one at any of the border crossings questioned her.

But now, with the sun high overhead, glaring down with all the force of hell, and the Colombian border far behind them, she'd reached her physical limit.

She stopped, too exhausted to go any farther.

Maxwell stirred, sat up straighter and looked at her. He licked his lips, the movement making her shiver in spite of her exhaustion. "Where are we?" he asked hoarsely.

The blood on his sleeve had dried, but there was too damn much of it. He looked rumpled and as sexy as hell. Exhausted though she was, she still noticed.

"Safe," she said, too tired to elaborate. She shut off the engine and leaned back in the seat. They were far enough from Colombia to call for backup. "We can get air support from here. Alexon has a private jet.'' She scrubbed a hand over her face. ''I suppose we should find a hotel or someplace to wait.'' The highway stretched out before them like a long dusty snake. There had to be some form of civilization a little farther up the road.

Maxwell groaned as he shifted in his seat. ''Sounds like a good plan to me. How you doing, Doc?''

The expression that claimed Maxwell's face sent a chill straight to Scout's bones. She released her own seat belt and turned around.

Kirstenof looked deathly still. She stared at him, holding her breath until she saw his thin chest lift frailly as he drew in a ragged inhalation of his own.

She and Maxwell were both out of their seats and opening the back doors of the vehicle in an instant.

''Dr. Kirstenof, are you okay?'' Scout asked softly, knowing full well that he was about as far from okay as was possible to get and still be breathing.

He shook his head once, so weakly that had she not been staring at him intently she would have missed it. ''I'm dying,'' he murmured.

Her gaze collided with Maxwell's.

''What's wrong, Doc? Was all the excitement too much for you?'' he suggested.

Scout hadn't thought of that. Maybe the scientist was having a heart attack. Okay, she knew CPR. She could help. She glanced around again. But where was the nearest hospital?

''Listen to me,'' Kirstenof said weakly. ''I don't have much time left.'' He pressed the satchel toward Scout. ''See that these papers and disks get to Alexon. They're your only hope for survival.''

She frowned, thinking that he must be confused. "I don't understand."

"My newest antidote is a failure...obviously," he said, then fell into a fit of coughing that she was certain he wouldn't survive.

"Just take it easy, Doc," Maxwell suggested. "Let us get you to a hospital. We can talk later."

"No!" Kirstenof protested with surprising strength. He grabbed Maxwell by the sleeve. "You have to listen now. I won't make it to a hospital."

Maxwell looked at Scout, then nodded at Kirstenof. "Go on."

"Two weeks ago I was inadvertently exposed to K-141. I wasn't too worried, since I was sure my newest antidote was a success. So I treated myself. I suffered no symptoms until two days ago."

Scout realized then that she had seen a drastic decline in Kirstenof's health in the past forty-eight hours, but hadn't had time to dwell on it.

"The rest of the antidote was destroyed with the lab, but the formula is in here." He patted the satchel she now held. "It's your only hope. Have Alexon's research team prepare the antidote immediately. It's too late for me, but perhaps it will postpone the inevitable until they can rectify whatever mistake I've made in my latest formula."

Scout's frown deepened. "I don't understand, Dr. Kirstenof. What are we trying to postpone?"

He looked at her then, his brown eyes watery with pain and regret. "Your death," he said quietly. "I've exposed you both to the virus."

Shock radiated through her. Her gaze flew immediately to Maxwell's. For one long beat they simply stared into each other's eyes.

"I'm very sorry," Kirstenof said. "You came here to help me and I've…" He looked from Scout to Maxwell. "You have two weeks at most. Make them correct the formula. Make them—"

He made a sound. One Scout recognized. She'd heard that same awful sound when her father had died—a kind of groan combined with one final, shuddering breath. And then he was gone.

Dr. Kirstenof was dead.

Scout met Maxwell's gaze.

And so were they.

MAX PACED THE FLOOR. He couldn't sit still. He glanced at Scout as he retraced his steps. They'd been in isolation for a full forty-eight hours and still no one had come to give them the temporary antidote Kirstenof had mentioned would delay the virus. No one had told them anything.

"What the hell are they doing?" he muttered.

Scout pushed up from the edge of her bed and looked around the room. There was a table with two chairs. A small kitchenette and two double beds. Behind one door was a bathroom. *Home sweet home,* Max thought irritably.

"I don't know. Nothing maybe." She sounded tired, defeated.

He wanted to reach out to her and tell her everything would be okay, but he was pretty sure it wouldn't be. Where was the vibrant, feisty young woman he'd met a couple days ago?

He almost laughed at himself. Being told you were going to die had that effect on people.

He turned around slowly in the middle of the room. Glass walls surrounded them on all sides. Lab technicians and scientists were observing them, he knew, but he couldn't see beyond the glass. Whatever lay beyond their transparent prison was blacked out. Those on the other side could see in, but he and Scout couldn't see out the darkened glass.

After the private plane had transported them to Alexon's main facility, they'd been allowed to shower, and had been provided with a clean change of clothes and, of course, food. Someone wearing a protective suit had patched up Max's arm where the bullet had grazed him. He'd been told that Victoria Colby had been briefed on his condition, but would not be allowed to see him. Since Alexon was just outside Chicago, he didn't understand the problem. But he supposed no one would be allowed into a level IV containment center except authorized personnel. Even the passenger compartment of the plane had been sealed off to protect the crew.

Scout had been informed that Harold Atkins was doing all he could to see that they were properly cared for.

Max wondered what difference it would make. If what Kirstenof had said was true, nothing mattered. Neither of them had slept for more than a few minutes since their arrival, but they hadn't talked much, either.

He looked at her now and wondered what it would be like to go out on a date with her. The attraction was certainly there. Maybe if circumstances had been different they could have…

But circumstances weren't different.

They were going to die.

"You know…" he began, feeling as if he had to say something. She looked so damned helpless and needy, standing there next to that bed. He was pretty sure she didn't have any family other than her uncle Harold, who wasn't really her uncle, just an old family friend. Not that having family would help, since she couldn't see them any more than he could see his own. But she looked so alone. He imagined he did, as well. "Maybe we could talk." He shrugged. "Get to know each other." After all, they had a few days left before…

Max shuddered inwardly. He didn't want to think about that. Dying at age thirty-three from some man-made virus that was supposed to be utilized only by the Defense Department was not exactly how he'd seen himself going.

Scout folded her arms across her chest and waltzed over to him, an odd look on her face.

"You want to talk?"

Taken aback by her peculiar tone, he shrugged again. "Why not? It's not like we're going any-where. We might as well make the best of our last days, right?"

"No one hates that things are going to end this way more than I do." She moved closer, the look he hadn't understood now becoming crystal clear. "But it appears we're screwed. I don't know about you, but I don't want to spend my last days on earth talking."

She looped her arms around his neck and his body went immediately hard. "I mean," she added, "it's not like we aren't attracted to each other."

A slow smile pulled one corner of his mouth up-ward. In that instant he knew his entire being had been waiting for this moment ever since he'd laid eyes on her. "Are you suggesting that we…"

She smiled back, that sexy twinkle in her eyes once more. "That's exactly what I'm suggesting."

Tension making it difficult to breathe, he glanced around at the glass walls. "You know they're watching us," he reminded her. Equal measures of need and desire were pumping through him so fast that he could hardly restrain himself.

She lifted one slender shoulder in a careless shrug. "Big deal. We're dead anyway, right?"

"Take a coffee break," Max said, glancing at those damnable glass walls once more. "This show's about to get X-rated." His gaze zeroed in on her lips then. "We're not dead yet," he murmured as his mouth followed the path his gaze had taken, sealing over hers in a kiss that went from slow and tender to hot and frantic in about two seconds.

Her taste, the feel of her in his arms, overwhelmed all other senses. Everything else faded into insignificance. There was only the one moment... and this woman.

At least they'd die happy.

Chapter Two

Four Months Later...

Max waited patiently in Victoria's office. She'd called him in on his first Saturday off in more than a month, but he didn't really mind. He preferred to stay busy. Especially now.

Despite his intention not to think about the past, it intruded all the same. Just four months ago he'd thought he was a dead man. The image of Scout Jackson immediately filled his mind. He'd barely known the woman, but the idea of her death had been immensely more painful to consider than that of his own. They'd known each other only a few days when...

The memory of making love while in mandatory isolation immediately sprang to mind. It hadn't mattered that they were being observed...they were going to die anyway, right?

Wrong.

For some reason that none of the Alexon scientists had been able to understand, both Max and Scout had been immune to the virus K-141. Max had no explanation and neither did Scout. It simply was. The antidote hadn't been necessary since natural antibodies had been detected in the blood tests Alexon had performed. Of course, they hadn't been told until the final days of isolation.

Alexon had insisted they stay in quarantine a full twenty-one days, during which time absolutely nothing happened—except a great physical relationship with a woman who'd proved to be every bit as assertive as he. It was the first time in his life that Max had been with a woman whose passion rivaled his own. Maybe it had simply been because they'd both thought they were going to die. He supposed that was something he would never know, since he hadn't seen Scout since the day they'd been released.

During their stay they'd endured dozens of blood tests and other analyses. Finally, when the powers that be were fully convinced the two were virus free, they had been allowed to go. Max's jaw clenched instantly at the memory. Scout Jackson had acted as if nothing had happened between them. As if making love with such abandon with a relative stranger for three weeks and then walking away was the norm.

Yet they were anything but strangers after those days in forced captivity. They'd known everything about each other. Max had to admit they'd spent almost as much time talking as they had making love.

Almost.

"Max," Amy Wells said breathlessly as she rushed into Victoria's office, jerking him back to the here and now.

He looked up and smiled. "Amy." She was filling in today for Mildred, Victoria's secretary. Mildred was spending time with her great-niece, whom she'd practically raised like a daughter. Mildred rarely took time off.

"I'm sorry you've had to wait. Victoria will be right with you. She and Ian had an unexpected conference call." Amy blushed. "I should have told you before you left your office, but I had several calls and—"

"It's okay," Max assured her. "I don't mind waiting."

Her smile winged back into place. "Can I get you anything while you wait?"

He shook his head as he moved toward the wall of windows to survey the view. "I'm fine. Thanks."

She nodded and backed out of the office.

Max shook his head again, this time at the thought of Amy. She was one of those young ladies who'd just gotten her first apartment, but still went home to Mom and Dad for dinner on Sundays. She'd never been in a serious relationship, and he imagined that the move to Chicago was as far as she'd ever been from the family farm, less than two hours away. Though more than competent at her job, she continually strove to do better. She'd recently been promoted from receptionist to personal assistant. Max had a feeling she had her sights set on becoming an investigator. And he could definitely see that happening. She was one tenacious young lady.

"Good morning, Max."

He looked up again, this time to see Victoria breezing through the door. She sent him a smile, one that could disarm any male breathing.

"Good morning, Victoria."

"I apologize for the delay." She skirted her desk and took a seat, then motioned for him to sit. "We have a slight dilemma this morning."

A rap on the open door drew Max's attention.

"You wanted to see me, Victoria?"

Doug Cooper stood in the doorway.

Max's frown was automatic. It wasn't that he didn't like the guy, but they just didn't see eye to eye on a few things. Primarily on how to proceed in any given situation while on assignment. Cooper had his way and Max had his own. It usually didn't cause a problem, except the one time they'd been teamed. Four months ago, in fact, when Max had been sent in to retrieve Scout and the Alexon scientist. Cooper had gotten annoyed because Max left him out of the loop at the last minute. It wasn't as if he'd intended to, but things had gone downhill fast, and Max had failed to let Cooper know when he left Colombia. Being shot and barely escaping rebels had played a large part in the oversight.

Judging by the look on Cooper's face when he noted Max's presence in Victoria's office, he hadn't forgotten that little episode, either.

"Yes. Douglas, have a seat."

Victoria smiled at her newest investigator. Though he hadn't had his first lead assignment yet, she appeared extremely pleased with his performance so far. Max felt immediately contrite. His problem with Cooper was more a personality clash than anything else. Max had been born in a blue-collar family. He'd worked his way through college and had earned every little thing in life. That a guy like Cooper could have the world handed to him on a silver platter and then still end up Max's equal annoyed him somehow. But he'd get over it. It wasn't Cooper's fault he'd been born to wealth any more than it was Max's that he hadn't. Not that he wished his life to be any different than it was, because he didn't.

Mainly, he just wanted to dislike the guy because he had it all without even trying.

Cooper, appearing every bit the J.F.K., Jr., look-alike from his savvy attire to his handsome mug, returned Victoria's smile and made himself comfortable in the chair next to Max.

He turned to Max then. "Good morning, Max," he said, that million dollar smile still in place.

"Cooper," Max acknowledged, purposely directing his attention back to Victoria without further ado.

"Gentlemen, we have somewhat of a dilemma," the boss said.

Both men sat up a little straighter and gave Victoria Colby their undivided attention.

"Regis Brandon from Alexon called me at home last night. They have a very serious situation. Harold Atkins, their head of security, was murdered two days ago, and Olivia Jackson is missing."

Max's pulse leaped into warp speed at the mention of Scout's name. She hated when people called her Olivia. "It sounds so girlie," she'd said. The rest of Victoria's statement sank in then.

…*Olivia Jackson is missing.*

Max leaned forward with the intention of demanding more information just as Victoria continued.

"Regis fears that Olivia may be involved somehow in the murder."

Max shook his head. "No way." Scout loved the guy like family. No way would she be involved in harming him. Murder was out of the question.

Victoria sighed and leaned back in her chair. "That's why I asked Douglas to join us," she said to Max. "I'm aware of your *personal* involvement with Miss Jackson and I'm not sure it would be a wise move to assign you to her case."

"Don't even think about giving this case to him," Max said curtly as he hitched a thumb in Cooper's direction. "No offense," he added as an afterthought. "But this is my case. We *were* personally involved," he said pointedly to Victoria. "We aren't now. That former involvement won't in any way lessen my ability to get the job done." He leveled his most unrelenting gaze on her. "I want this assignment."

The boss studied him for a long moment before speaking. "Max, I know a great deal about allowing personal involvement to override good judgment. More than you can imagine. And I also know that whether you're involved with her right now or not, you still have strong feelings where she is concerned." Victoria held up a hand to stop him when Max would have argued his point further. "I do, however, know you well enough to believe that you will do the job right. So I'm going to let you have the case."

Relief rushed through him. He relaxed visibly.

"With one stipulation," she clarified.

Max tensed once more.

"You will keep Douglas in the loop. He will

know your every move. If he for one moment believes that you've lost your objectivity, he takes over. Agreed?''

Max glanced at the man sitting silently beside him, then exhaled a heavy breath and turned back to Victoria. ''Agreed.''

She nodded, then continued with the briefing. ''Regis feels you would be best suited for this assignment in any event,'' she said to Max, her eyes allowing him to see the degree to which she disagreed with that conclusion. ''He believes that the only way to draw Olivia out is by using someone she trusts.'' Victoria considered Max a moment. ''He is evidently convinced that since the two of you had a physical relationship, Miss Jackson will trust you.''

Max shrugged. ''The point's valid. The decision to go our separate ways was mutual. We didn't part enemies or even angry with each other. We were both too glad to be alive to harbor resentment for anything that happened during that three-week period of quarantine.''

''I agree,'' Cooper interjected.

Max resisted the urge to look his way. He didn't need anyone else to tell him what he felt, now or then.

''I was present when Miss Jackson and Max said their goodbyes. I'm certain she not only trusted him, but also had strong feelings for him.''

Max did look at Cooper then. How the hell could he know that for sure? Even Max had doubted how Scout really felt about him in the end. He knew for certain how far he'd fallen for her during those twenty-one days, but he hadn't been absolutely sure if the depth of feeling was mutual. Still wasn't. In fact, he figured she'd gone back to her ex-boyfriend. The one she'd broken off with just days before going on the Colombian mission. Max gritted his teeth as the name filtered through his mind. Gage something or other.

"Considering that her pseudo-uncle is dead and that she had no other family," Cooper continued, "Max is probably the only person she would trust."

The reality that Scout might be all alone out there, and facing a possible murder charge for a crime she couldn't have committed, hit Max with the force of a physical blow.

"All right," Victoria announced, once more dragging him to attention. She reached across her desk, offering him the case file. The manila folder was considerably thicker this time. "You'll find all the details in here. There isn't that much you don't already know. The two new details are Harold's murder and the fact that Alexon insists that the murder stems from Miss Jackson's having stolen something that belongs to the company. Harold was apparently trying to retrieve it when he was murdered."

Max shook his head again. That was impossible. Scout wasn't a thief and she damn sure wasn't a murderer. The only way she would kill someone would be in self-defense. So unless her uncle was attempting to kill her, she wouldn't have killed him. Max swore under his breath.

"Max, we would appreciate it if you shared your thoughts on the matter," Victoria said with a directness that left no doubt about her loss of patience. "It's obvious you're having difficulty with the details as I've outlined them."

Now she was annoyed with him. Not that he could blame her. He'd just assured her that he would keep Cooper informed, and here he was keeping things to himself before he even got out of her office.

"It's just that I know she wouldn't kill her uncle." He shrugged, at a loss to completely relay how he could know that with such certainty. "She's not a thief and she's definitely not a killer. There has to be something else going on that we're not aware of." He looked straight at Victoria then. "How well do you know this Regis Brandon? Could he be hiding something?"

Victoria spread her hands. "Anything's possible. Regis has been the head of Alexon for two years now. He has a stellar reputation, but that doesn't eliminate the possibility that he could be dirty on some level. One never knows what a person is capable of...until you dig deeply enough"

Touché, Max acknowledged silently.

After the briefing, he exited Victoria's office, already mentally ticking off possible scenarios for Scout's predicament. Victoria's warning kept echoing in his head. *One never knows just what a person is capable of....* But he did know Scout; he knew every inch of her. But did he really *know* her other than in the biblical sense?

"Look, Max," Cooper said, coming up beside him.

Max turned toward him, admitting that he likely still owed the guy an apology for the last time the two had worked a case involving Scout.

"I didn't ask for this," Cooper explained, apparently feeling the need to justify his inclusion. "I told Victoria you could handle the situation."

Max heaved another of those long, drawn-out breaths. This was mostly his fault. "Cooper, I was wrong before. I left you out of the loop just like Victoria said. It won't happen this time." He offered his hand. "And for the record, I'm certain you didn't try to horn in on my case. I know Victoria. She makes her own decisions based on fact and gut instinct. So we're clear, all right?"

Cooper gave his hand a firm shake. "Clear."

"Let's meet in a couple of hours to discuss strategy," Max suggested before walking away. This time he would give Cooper that chance he'd denied him before.

That was one thing Max could safely say about himself: when he was wrong, he admitted it.

He hoped like hell he wasn't wrong about Scout.

MAX STOOD BACK from the crowd, observing, analyzing each elegantly dressed attendee and keeping an eye out for one person in particular. Perpetrators often showed up at the funerals of their victims just to get the final laugh. Not that he thought for one second that Scout was the perp. He did, however, expect her to show.

The funeral had taken place in one of Chicago's premier cathedrals, with all the elaborate trimmings. In the past twenty-four hours, Max and Cooper had learned that Harold Atkins had no family other than Scout, and really had no close friends other than work associates. But Alexon had gone all-out for his funeral. The arrangements were nothing short of lavish.

Now, as the brief graveside service reached its conclusion, there still had been no sign of Scout or anyone who looked or behaved suspiciously. Unless she'd watched the event with high-powered binoculars from a safe distance away, Scout wasn't around. Max was relatively sure she hadn't done that because Cooper was doing that very thing, and he hadn't seen hide nor hair of the lovely fugitive.

Scout's private investigations business was located in Houston, Texas, but Max felt certain she would be close by for her uncle's funeral. Though he hadn't caught sight of her, he wasn't ready to admit defeat just yet, either. He was still certain she would show…eventually. He scanned the grand old cemetery yet again. The elite of Chicago were buried here. His gaze drifted back to the gathered crowd. Those in attendance ranged from the mayor to well-known local entrepreneurs. Nothing but the best for a mere chief of security? Max found that unsettling. It was just one more element that didn't fit, any more than the idea that Scout had committed the crime. But, he imagined, these people had likely come to show their support for one of their own—Regis Brandon, CEO of Alexon.

Upon checking on Scout's business in Houston, Cooper had found out from her assistant that Scout had done nothing more than call in to her office for weeks now. The assistant was concerned that something was wrong, but had followed orders to refer new cases to other agencies, taking only those that she could handle herself right from the office. According to the assistant, at this rate Scout would be out of business before the end of the year, and it was September already.

Max remembered the story Scout had told him about how she'd come to be a P.I., and he couldn't see her letting go so easily. Her father and her uncle had originally started the business after retiring from the military about eight years back. Then, two years ago, her father had passed away and her uncle had semi-retired, choosing the posh job with Alexon over continuing to work the private investigations field without his friend and partner. Scout considered the business all that she had left of her father, and had decided to take it over herself. She'd been working cases between college classes, anyway.

She was a crackerjack investigator, she'd bragged, and a hell of a recovery agent. Max could see her going after some big guy who'd jumped bail. The thought made him smile despite his somber surroundings.

He'd also learned that ever since her mother had died, when Scout was really young, she'd traveled a lot with her father, during his military days. Like Max, she'd lived in Colombia for three of those years. During their twenty-one days in quarantine, they'd learned that they had a lot in common aside from physical chemistry.

Max frowned. Why had he simply let her walk away? He'd disciplined himself not to think about her all this time—well, most of it, anyway. But now he was asking himself all kinds of questions, and he had no answers. He should have tried harder to change her mind about going back to Texas, or at least attempted to pursue a long-distance relationship.

But he hadn't. And now she was in trouble.

Could he have prevented this from happening if

he'd been there for her? Or would he have just been in the way when she and her ex-boyfriend reunited? Max clenched his jaw at the thought.

God, he was a wreck. He had to stop analyzing the past, and focus on the present. It was the only way he could help Scout now. Whether she'd gone back to the other guy or not, he had to help her.

"Heads up." Cooper's voice echoed in his earpiece. "We've got a dark trench coat on the move at two o'clock."

Max looked slightly to his right until he had the subject in view. Female for sure, he decided, noting the toned legs and high heels beneath the concealing trench coat. He was on the move even as he assimilated the data, heading in that direction.

Men and women, most dressed in black, were wandering away from the burial site, moving into his path. Max deftly dodged each intrusion, gaining speed with every step.

"I'm on the ground and headed your way," Cooper informed him.

"Almost on her," Max murmured, moving faster and faster.

She hadn't looked back, and was practically running herself now. But Max was faster.

Two more seconds…and he had her.

He grabbed her by the forearm and whirled her around to face him, simultaneously skidding to a halt.

Breathing hard and ready to shake her for running, he stared down into her face, looking beyond the big hat and dark glasses she'd used as camouflage.

A stranger.

"What are you doing?" the woman demanded, jerking free of his hold. She flashed a personnel badge. "I'm from the *Tribune*. I have a right to be here. You can't keep the press out of a breaking news event."

Max closed his eyes and blew out a breath. Dammit. It wasn't her. Just a damn reporter.

"Sorry," he said. He backed off, giving the angry lady some space. "I thought you were someone else."

She glared at him, then spun on her heel and rushed away.

Cooper emerged from a nearby copse of trees. "Sorry, Max. I couldn't see her face. And she was practically running away from the service." He shrugged. "Looked suspicious to me."

"It's okay. I thought the same thing."

"I guess our lady's a no-show," Cooper suggested as he glanced around the cemetery.

Max scrubbed a hand over his face, vaguely noting that it was only two-thirty and already he had five o'clock stubble. "So far, anyhow," he said, more to himself than to Cooper.

"You think she still might put in an appearance?"

Max considered that for a moment, then, without reservation, said, "Yes. She'll be here. She loved this guy. Saying goodbye is something she'll have to do."

"Well, then. I'll get back to my post."

Max shook his head. "I think I can handle this for now. With the crowd gone, she'll stand out like a sore thumb if she shows. You go back to the office and get in touch with her assistant again. Find out if Scout has called in." Max considered for a bit before continuing. "I've got a better idea." He met Cooper's expectant gaze. "I want you to go down to Houston and interview the assistant in person. She may be holding out on us. If anyone knows where Scout is, it'll be her."

"Good call," Cooper allowed, stroking his chin thoughtfully. "I'd like to check out Miss Jackson's apartment, as well. I'll let you know the moment I have anything worth passing on."

Max watched him go, having no doubt that his colleague would learn whatever the receptionist knew, and find anything worth finding at Scout's apartment. Scout's assistant wouldn't stand a chance against Cooper's sophisticated charm. If he couldn't get the truth out of her, no one could.

After walking the cemetery grounds once more for good measure, Max selected a vantage point high on a hillside to watch for Scout. As he settled in for a long evening of surveillance, he took solace in one thing: she would be here. There was no two ways about it.

Scout would come to pay her respects.

And he would be waiting.

Chapter Three

Scout waited a full hour after darkness fell before making her move. If the cops or any of Alexon's secret security team were out there they'd have to be using night vision binoculars to see her. But then, she didn't discount that possibility, since Alexon's team was highly trained and well equipped. This wasn't your typical security detail. These guys were far more mercenary than your retired cop moonlighting to make an extra buck, or some dude on a power trip trying to use the uniform to get dates.

No, these were the kind of professionals a smart person avoided at all costs. Unfortunately, right now Scout couldn't do smart. Her chin trembled at the thought of her uncle Harold. Though he wasn't her 'real uncle, she couldn't have loved him more if he had been. For as long as she could remember he'd been a part of her life. He'd been there for her at age twelve when her father had gone on a mission where military dependents weren't allowed, and he'd stood by her two years ago when her father had been murdered and her whole world had collapsed.

Harold Atkins had been her rock. He was the only

family she had left in the world and now he was gone.

Scout blinked back burning tears. She focused on the present, pushing all other thoughts away. Harold was dead. Though she hadn't seen the killer's face, she would lay money on his being a member of Alexon's watchdog commandos. He'd ruthlessly murdered Harold right before her eyes. She herself had barely escaped capture. Only two things mattered to her at this point: bringing the person responsible for Harold's death to justice, and protecting herself.

To protect herself was to safeguard the tiny life growing inside her. Coming here was a risk to her and the baby, that was true. But it was the only way to catch the killer. If she simply disappeared, then justice would never be served. She would see to that, if nothing else, then she would disappear.

Hard as she tried, she had been unable as of yet to solve her father's homicide. But she'd been out of the loop where his professional life was concerned. It was different this time. She was involved, knew the whole deal. And she'd witnessed the murder. Even if she hadn't seen the killer's face, she would never forget the way he moved or the sound of his voice.

With the stealth she'd learned from the master himself—her father—she moved through the cemetery, weaving between the rows of massive monuments and more discreet headstones. The glow from the full moon made the white carnations blanketing Harold's fresh grave gleam briefly before the clouds obscured the light once more. The cloudy night would work to her advantage. Like a conductor leading a symphony, she directed her respiration to a slow, steady rate, ordered her heart's rhythm to a calmer pace and kept her body's movements fluid. Any sudden move would draw attention to her position.

Scout wanted the element of surprise on her side. It was necessary, since there was only one of her and probably a half-dozen of the other guys.

Her plan wasn't perfect, but if it got her close enough to Harold's killer, he was going to fully understand the eye-for-an-eye theory of revenge. All she wanted was him, and then she was out of here. The retreat would be tricky, but she'd done tricky before. She'd spent the entire day yesterday studying this cemetery. Every grave marker, every tree and bench were familiar to her, each location firmly imprinted on her memory. She'd lead her pursuers on a merry chase and she would get away for two reasons: overconfidence and mandatory restraint. They outnumbered her, so they would automatically assume she'd be an easy target, thus the overconfidence. Specific orders had been given that she was to be returned to Alexon *unharmed,* therefore the restraint.

Scout moved into more treacherous territory now. She skirted one last headstone and stepped into the small open area where her uncle had been buried. This was the newest section of the cemetery, with only a few graves and no trees—meaning no cover to speak of.

If anyone waited for her in the darkness, he would see her now.

Minutes ticked by, the night sounds seeming to grow louder with each passing second. A September breeze whispered through the leaves of the trees a few yards away, ushering toward her the scents of evergreens and freshly turned earth. Her gaze drifted down to her uncle's final resting place, and the sting of tears assaulted her once more.

He'd tried to protect her and he'd paid with his life.

Now she had no one. She flattened one trembling hand against her still-flat belly. But that would change in a few months. All she had to do was keep herself and this baby safe. Another image flitted through the back of her thoughts: of sandy-blond hair and blue eyes and a body to die for.

Scout shook off thoughts of Pierce Maxwell. He was the last complication she needed in her life.

He'd walked away four months ago without looking back. So she'd done the same. But he could have at least called. She'd almost called him...once. Scout barely caught herself before she sighed. Oh well, it was too late now, anyway. He'd likely forgotten all about her.

There wasn't much chance she'd be forgetting him. But, she reminded herself, her memories of him were most likely overblown. They'd spent those intense hours in the jungle together, and he had risked his life to save hers and Dr. Kirstenof's. The whole hero scenario had probably blinded her to the reality that he was just a guy. Three weeks of forced isolation in his company instantly whizzed through her mind like a video on Fast Forward. Okay, he was more than just a guy. He was...

The rustle of grass to her right jerked her back to the here and now.

About time.

Scout eased into position, drawing her weapon from her waistband at the small of her back. Gun in hand, she stayed absolutely still for three more beats. Nothing. Not a single sound.

What the hell were they waiting for? They'd have to be idiots or blind not to know she was right in front of them, barely concealed by the one large headstone in this section of the cemetery.

She listened intently for the slightest audible movement. Leaves tumbled across the grass, drawing her gaze to the right, where autumn's first cast-offs swirled, then lodged against the grave markers blocking their path. The varying sizes and shapes of the tombstones created unearthly shadows in the faint moonlight, giving a sinister feel. A bat dipped wildly, then zoomed upward to the protective canopy of the nearby trees.

Scout frowned. This wasn't right, somehow. Any investigator or operations strategist worth his salt would anticipate her appearance at the cemetery to pay her respects to her uncle.

Alexon wouldn't just give up, write her off.

They wanted her… No, that wasn't exactly right. They wanted—

A hand clamped over her mouth at the same instant another one manacled her right wrist, so her weapon dangled uselessly. Scout's heart nearly stopped, then pounded fiercely against her sternum.

"Don't—"

In a single instant Scout noted two things and accomplished another. This guy didn't have his weapon drawn, since he was using both hands on her, and secondly, her left arm was free. Before he could utter another word she slammed her left elbow into his gut and wrenched away from him.

He still managed to hang on to her right wrist. Sacrificing the weapon, she dropped it and twisted out of his hold, then ran like hell.

"Wait!"

The male voice almost made her hesitate… almost. She pushed forward. Zigzagged between headstones, even jumped over a few. Still he was right behind her.

"Scout!"

Hesitation slowed her.

She knew that voice.

It couldn't be—

A heavy body slammed into hers. She lost her balance and they tumbled to the ground in a tangle of arms and legs. She tried to roll free, but he trapped her there. Fear seared through her. Alexon had given orders that she wasn't to be harmed, but that didn't guarantee she was entirely safe. And where were the others? She was looking for one guy in particular and this wasn't him. She was sure of it. She couldn't be caught yet.

Renewed determination roared through her veins and the fear evaporated. She wasn't going down easily. Fighting like a wildcat, Scout kicked and clawed for freedom.

Her assailant swore. The sound of his voice nagged at her again. Her mind raced with the concept that this might be—

"Dammit, Scout! Stop fighting!" He grunted when the toe of her shoe make contact with his shin. "It's me! Max!"

Max.

Relief very nearly overwhelmed her and she went still.

"Are you going to behave yourself now?" he demanded, sounding none too happy.

There wasn't enough light to make out his features, but Scout could imagine those blue eyes glaring at her, that full mouth set in a grim line. Then a new kind of uneasiness erupted inside her.

This was not good.

The last thing she needed was Pierce Maxwell involved in all this. There were things he didn't know. Couldn't know. The uneasiness abruptly morphed into full-fledged fear. Alexon had sent him. She knew it as surely as she knew her own name. Alexon, or more precisely her uncle as head of security, had hired the Colby Agency to find her once before.

Why else would Max be involved?

He had no way of knowing all the circumstances....

He was one of them.

"Get off me!" She shoved at his mile-wide chest. "Now!" she demanded when he gave no indication that he intended to act immediately.

"As soon as I have your word that you won't do anything we'll both regret," he countered, his own voice demanding.

Heat was already pooling in her lower anatomy. How could her traitorous body react so quickly and insistently to the enemy? The idea made her furious.

"I said get off me!" She had her knee between his muscular thighs before he could react, but she stopped short of making full contact with her target. "Or else," she threatened.

Evidently knowing she was serious, he rose up on all fours, effectively freeing her from the prison his strong body made. "Just don't do anything rash," he reminded her. "I'm here to help you."

Scout scrambled away from him, but didn't run for it as she'd intended. She would hear him out; she owed him that, she supposed. Besides, he might be working for the enemy, but Max wasn't a bad guy.

"Did Alexon send you?" The question rang out between them with all the sharpness and accusation she'd intended. "If you're working for them we have nothing to discuss."

She folded her arms over her chest and glared in his direction—for all the good it would do in the darkness.

Max didn't want to risk hurting her. Manhandling her was the last thing he'd intended. He'd only meant to catch her off guard, since she was armed, and to ensure the least ruckus possible in case anyone was following either of them. Alexon had warned him that one of their competitors was on Scout's trail, as well.

"Are you all right?" he asked, unable to concentrate completely until he had the answer to that. He couldn't make out her face very well in the dark, but he'd felt her desperation in every toned muscle of her body. She was scared. What bothered him the most was that she obviously considered him to be aligned with the enemy.

"I'm just dandy," she retorted. "My uncle is dead and I'm on the run from his killer. I'd call that dandy, wouldn't you?"

He frowned. She thought someone in Alexon had

killed her uncle? Or maybe she was referring to the competitor. Max reached out to her, but she jerked away from his touch. He couldn't understand why her reaction pained him so, but it did.

"I'm really sorry about your uncle," he said softly, knowing he had to say that regardless of what she thought of him. "Victoria asked me to pass along her condolences, as well." He heard the little catch in Scout's breath and his gut clenched. Here she was, sneaking around in a dark cemetery, trying to pay her respects to her uncle, and Max was supposed to take custody of her.

What did that make him?

The enemy.

"Thank you," she managed to answer, her voice wobbling a bit. "Now, what did they hire you to do? Are you supposed to bring me in or just shoot me where I stand?"

Her words stunned him. Did she really believe he would hurt her in any way? She had to know he wouldn't. She had to know the Colby Agency didn't do that kind of work. Neither did Alexon, to his knowledge.

"I just want to talk to you," he assured her quietly. He could feel her withdrawing. Instinct told him she'd make a run for it before she'd let him take her in. "Can we go somewhere and talk? Somewhere quiet and safe? You pick the place," he offered, hoping to allay her fears.

"What do you want to talk about?" she demanded, uncertainty underscoring her cocky tone.

For a moment before he responded, he thought about what he should say. He needed her full attention. He needed her open to the options he intended to offer. To achieve that, he needed to make her see just how precarious her position was.

He edged closer. When she heard what he had to say she might just bolt. "We need to talk about why Alexon thinks you murdered your uncle."

If he'd slapped her, Scout wouldn't have been any more surprised. How could anyone think she'd killed her uncle? It was insane. Beyond insane...

Her heart was pounding again, her pulse throbbing so hard she was certain a heart attack was imminent. Her breath all but stalled in her lungs.

She had not killed her uncle.

But, she realized, ice filling her veins, she couldn't prove she hadn't. She'd been the last person besides the murderer to see him alive.

"I didn't kill him," she said with more strength than she'd considered herself capable of. Surely Max didn't believe that lie. He knew her better than that. She thought of the days they'd spent together in isolation and the way she'd gone back to rescue him after getting Dr. Kirstenof to safety. Max had to know she wouldn't murder a man in cold blood.

"I believe you," he said, his voice quietly reassuring. "But there are others who aren't so sure. We need to clear up this situation before it gets completely out of control." He eased closer. "Let me help you."

The urge to run nearly overpowered her desire to trust him.

She was so tired. She needed time to grieve, but she couldn't. Keeping her baby safe was all that mattered anymore. But how could she do that if Alexon convinced the police she was guilty of murder? There was only her word against the killer's.

She'd been at the scene and had run away. It didn't take a rocket scientist to trump up motive.

She was screwed.

Big time.

Her gaze sought Max in the darkness. She could make out his form, the outline of his face, but not his eyes. The realization that they stood alone in the middle of the cemetery was immensely telling. Alexon had sent him to find her, to bring her in. They trusted him enough to back off and let him do the job.

That was not good…at least not from her vantage point.

Instead of backing away herself, or making a run for it, knowing that he would only catch her, she stood her ground. He was faster than her and out-weighed her by a good seventy or eighty pounds, so running would be pointless. If she only had her weapon…

"If you believe me, then why are you armed when I'm not?" Scout held perfectly still while he contemplated her question. She didn't even breathe. If he wanted her to believe him badly enough he'd make a show of faith. She almost smiled. In about ten seconds she'd have him. Her father had taught her this trick and it always worked, unless, of course, the other party involved was a lowlife scum-bag criminal. And that wasn't the case at all.

"I tell you what," he said congenially, "I'll put my weapon right over here on this headstone, out of reach, and then we'll talk. That sound okay to you?"

She nodded, then remembered that he couldn't see her. "Your backup piece, too," she told him, remembering the ankle holster he'd worn four months ago.

"No problem." Max placed his weapon on the headstone, then crouched down to retrieve the other one. "I want us to be on equal footing here, Scout. I'm not the enemy. I want—"

Knowing he could easily stop her with the backup piece and, at the same time, knowing he wouldn't dare shoot her, she grabbed the nine-millimeter from the headstone. Her fingers instantly curled into position.

"Give me your keys," she ordered as she pressed the barrel of the weapon to his forehead. He'd already snagged his backup gun, but she knew he wouldn't use it.

He shook his head, the movement clear despite the sparse moonlight cutting through the clouds. "Don't do this, Scout."

"Give me your keys," she repeated hotly. "Don't think I won't use this."

He laughed softly, but, to his credit, wasn't fool enough to move. "No you won't. You didn't go back into that jungle to rescue me four months ago only to shoot me tonight."

"Things are different now," she said pointedly. "There's a possibility I killed my uncle, or have you forgotten?"

His sigh was audible. "Let me help you."

It was so tempting. But how could she be sure she could trust him? Alexon had hired him. Alexon was the enemy. Max didn't understand the kind of people he was dealing with.

And he didn't know…the other. It was best if he didn't.

"If you want to help me, give me your keys," she repeated.

Just then the clouds parted and moonlight cut through the darkness, revealing the intensity on Max's face.

"The only way you're walking out of here without me is if you shoot me," he said, determination glinting in those luminous blue eyes. "And I know that isn't going to happen."

Scout firmed her resolve and cocked the weapon. "You sure about that?" Raising one eyebrow in a skeptical tilt, she added, "Remember, I'm desperate." She pressed the barrel a little harder against his skin, flinching inside with the effort it took. "Now give me those keys." She had a rental and didn't need his vehicle, but she didn't want him following her.

He shook his head. "No dice."

She released a mighty breath and firmed her grip on the weapon. "Well, I guess that leaves me no choice."

Chapter Four

Olivia Scout Jackson was a lot of things, but a good liar she wasn't.

She wouldn't shoot him.

Even if Max hadn't known her as well as he did, the truth glittered in those gray eyes. Yes, he saw the desperation, but above all else he saw the vulnerability and fear.

There was no way she had been involved in anyone's murder.

"Let me help you," Max murmured softly. "You know you can trust me."

For three long beats she didn't move. She stood there, staring down at him with that damn weapon boring into his skull. Just when he was certain she wasn't going to trust him, she relaxed and blew out a disgusted breath.

"Don't make me regret this," she said curtly as she lowered the weapon, disengaged it, then offered it to him butt first.

Max pushed himself to his feet as he accepted the nine-millimeter. "I won't," he assured her.

She still didn't look convinced. But she had good reason. Her uncle was dead and people were after her. He didn't know the whole story yet, but those two things alone were enough to make anyone jumpy.

Her gaze locked with his as he shoved his gun into his shoulder holster. "So what happens now?" she asked.

He glanced around the deserted cemetery. Alexon had assured him that they would not interfere, and he hoped like hell they stuck by their word. He needed her to trust him. It was the only way he'd get the unvarnished truth.

"We go someplace safe to talk." He placed his hand against her arm and urged her forward, heading toward where she'd dropped her weapon. "You tell me what's going on and then we figure out where to go from there."

She laughed dryly. "You won't believe me."

Max paused to look at her through the darkness. The clouds had obscured the moon once more. "Try me."

She didn't respond, just felt around for her lost weapon and tucked it into the waistband of her jeans when she finally found it.

"We'll do it your way then," she agreed. "For now. As long as you promise not to turn me in to Alexon until you've heard my side."

He agreed and showed her the way to his SUV. But she hesitated before getting in. "What about my rental?"

According to the data Alexon had given him, there was no record of her flying from Houston to Chicago. They weren't sure how long she'd been in the area; they only knew that she had ground trans-portation. When they'd checked with the rental agencies, however, they'd come up with zilch. If she'd rented locally, she hadn't used her own name. Max wasn't surprised at that. Scout was too smart for that kind of bad move.

"We'll come back for it," he said in answer to her question. He waved his hand toward the open door of his SUV. "I don't want to risk you changing your mind about trusting me." Might as well be honest up front, he decided. She'd see through anything else.

The dim glow cast by the vehicle's interior light captured her half smile. "I'm very resourceful, Maxwell," she retorted, using his surname for emphasis. "If I decide I can't trust you, I won't need my rental to blow you off."

Max closed the door behind her and quickly skirted the hood to climb behind the wheel.

"Where are we going?" she asked as he started the engine and turned on the headlights.

"My place."

He didn't elaborate. She would find out soon enough that blowing him off wouldn't be so easy where they were going. Max smiled to himself at the idea of just how frustrated she would be when they arrived at the intended destination.

The narrow lane twisted around the perimeter of the cemetery, finally widening as it neared the entry gate. Max glanced first left, then right before easing out onto the street. The drive to his place would take about forty-five minutes. Maybe he could get a few answers on the way. He needed to know two things right away: what had she taken from Alexon and why was she running?

Though he couldn't imagine Scout stealing anything, there had to be some reason why she was on the run. He couldn't really see any point in Alexon making up that kind of story. It was a high-profile company with a stellar reputation. This kind of thing seemed entirely out of character. But then so did murder and thievery where Scout was concerned.

Once on the road headed to Crystal Lake, he decided to simply ask her what Alexon thought she'd taken. When he glanced toward the passenger seat, the words never made it past his lips. She was asleep. Or at least she appeared to be. He could only guess how long she'd gone without rest or food or both. His gut clenched at the thought that she was obviously exhausted. As much as he wanted to know what was going on, he wanted to take care of her first.

Maybe Alexon was wrong and Victoria was right. Maybe he wasn't the man for this job.

SCOUT AWOKE SUDDENLY.

She straightened in her seat.

The car had stopped moving—that's what had awakened her.

It was still dark outside.

Where was she?

She followed the beam of headlights to the A-frame house nestled amid the trees. Max stepped into her line of vision as he climbed the steps leading up to the deck.

Glancing around, she could just make out the dim shapes of trees. They were in the woods. Deep in the woods, the best she could tell in the faint moonlight. Wherever they were, she'd never been here before, and she didn't like that. Instantly her heart rate shifted into high gear.

A knock on the window only inches from her face made her jump. She glared at Max, who waited outside her door. Exhaustion was taking its toll on her, making it hard to gather her composure and get her bearings. She needed food and more sleep. But could she really trust this man to keep her safe while she slept through the night?

She swallowed tightly. Well, she'd trusted him this far. She opened the door and slid out of the SUV. She could give him the benefit of the doubt for a little longer.

"Welcome to my castle," he said with a magnanimous wave of his arm. "Go on inside and make yourself at home. I'll be right in."

He'd turned on the exterior lights, she noticed as she made her way toward the deck. The headlights behind her went out and the engine died. As she ascended the steps, the sound of a vehicle door closing echoed, and two seconds later Max jogged up next to her.

She didn't glance at him when he opened the front door to the house. He waited, allowing her to go inside first. When he'd closed the door behind them, she finally looked at him. He armed the security system and gave her a reassuring smile.

"The bedroom is at the top of the stairs. Have a nap or a shower if you'd like. I'll rustle up something to eat."

Did she look that bad or was she simply that easy to read? Determined not to spurn his kindness, and to trust him until she had reason not to, she offered a halfhearted smile. "I'd love a shower." Though she didn't have a change of clothes with her, a long, hot shower would relax her tense muscles.

"Make yourself at home," he called over his shoulder as he headed toward what she presumed to be the kitchen.

Before going upstairs Scout took a moment to familiarize herself with her surroundings. The front door opened into one large room. Log-and-chink walls and hardwood floors glowed, warm and inviting. The ceiling soared upward, to where a second-floor balcony overlooked the expansive room below. The furnishings were on the Spartan side, few and simple, but comfortable looking nonetheless.

She moved in the direction she'd watched Max go and peeked at the small but efficient kitchen. On the other side of the enormous living area was a small powder room. The only exterior doors were the one they'd entered, adjacent to the staircase, and the one she noted in the kitchen. Her gaze roamed up the staircase. There would be windows up there, but no door, she imagined. Unless there was a second-story deck on the back of the house.

Having seen all she needed to downstairs, she followed the path her gaze had taken, climbing the stairs slowly, mostly because she was totally spent.

The bedroom was large as well. Though it, too, was sparsely furnished, it did have lots of great exercise equipment. Scout moved around the room, allowing her fingers to glide over the smooth surfaces of the various machines. She was impressed. No wonder Max had such a great body. She could see him working out every night before bed, or maybe every morning before his shower. Either way, her mind immediately conjured the image of him completely naked. She shivered and banished the picture. She had to keep her attention off that. She was in enough trouble already.

There was no second-floor deck, which meant no escape route from up here, unless she wanted to risk jumping, and she didn't. Maybe if circumstances were different she might take that kind of chance to evade capture. But she wouldn't risk her baby to save herself.

She stilled next to the huge four-poster bed that claimed one side of the room. No matter what else happened, she had to make sure he didn't find out about the baby. She closed her eyes and forced back the little voice that wanted to argue with that decision. She couldn't risk it. If he found out…

Exiling those thoughts, she moved into the bathroom and stripped off her clothes, placing her weapon carefully on the marble vanity top. She stroked the locket she always wore and decided that Max didn't need to know about the baby. He wouldn't understand. She was certain of that.

What he didn't know wouldn't hurt him. In fact, now that she thought about it, she realized the knowledge might even put him in danger.

That decision made, Scout stepped beneath the hot spray of water and closed her eyes, effectively pushing away all thought, reveling in the feel of the water sluicing over her skin. All she had to do was relax, eat and maybe even get some rest. If Alexon had hired Max to find her, then perhaps that's why they had backed off. They would wait and let him bring her in. That could work to her advantage. She could take a little time to regroup and plot a new strategy. If nothing else, she was relatively sure she could keep Max from turning her over for a day or two, anyway.

All she had to do was keep him from learning the truth.

If he believed her when she told him Alexon's own people had killed her uncle, then maybe he would help her disappear. But she couldn't disappear until she'd taken down the man who'd killed her uncle. She wasn't leaving another murder unsolved. Not when she had witnessed it with her own eyes. Not when she couldn't get that voice out of her head. If Max didn't want to help her, she'd do it on her own.

In the kitchen, Max spread the array of cold cuts on the counter and reached back into the fridge for the mayo and mustard. He remembered from their stay under observation that she hated mayo and loved cheese, any and all kinds. So he piled her sandwich high with three different cheeses and twice that many meats. He kept a variety of sandwich fixings available, since he rarely had the time or inclination to cook. Lettuce, no tomato and extra pickles. He topped off the mountain of fillings with a second slice of sourdough bread and garnished it with his favorite pitted olives on the side.

After preparing his own sandwich, he placed both plates on a tray, grabbed a bag of chips and snagged two beers from the fridge. He'd just placed the laden tray on the dining table when Scout descended the stairs.

She wore the same clothes, but her hair was damp from a shower. She looked good. Too good. Already he had experienced some major difficulty keeping his hands away from her. He wanted to touch her.

Her skin was as smooth and pale as cream. The blackness of her hair stood out in such stark contrast that it never failed to draw his attention. But the dark circles under her eyes reminded him of the loss she had recently suffered, and he chastised himself for allowing his thoughts to go down that path. She didn't need a lover right now, she needed a friend. And he wanted desperately to be that for her.

He'd be lying if he said he wasn't still attracted to her physically. He had been since the day he'd first laid eyes on her in that jungle. In their forced isolation and with the certainty of death hanging over their heads, that attraction had mushroomed with all the force of a nuclear blast. And they'd talked…some. He knew she was alone in the world since her uncle's death. She had no living relatives. Too busy in her P.I. and bounty-hunter business to make many friends, she had no one to turn to.

Gage.

Her ex-boyfriend's name zoomed into the middle of his thoughts. Max tensed instantly. Who was to say she'd been alone these past four months?

With his jaw clenched so hard he could scarcely speak, he gestured to the table and said, "You should eat." He'd suddenly lost his own appetite. It happened every single time he thought of the guy, and he didn't even know him! Fury whipped through Max at his own stupidity.

Scout glanced at the food. "Do you have any milk?"

A scowl furrowed Max's forehead. She liked that kind of beer, he was certain. They had discussed how much they'd wanted one when they'd thought they were spending their last days on this earth. She'd been the one to bring it up.

"Sure," he said tightly, and headed back to the kitchen to get her a glass of milk. He hesitated at the counter, glass in hand, and cursed himself for behaving so irrationally. This jealousy he felt for a man he didn't even know was totally out of line. She might not even be involved with the guy anymore. Then again, their own time together might have been nothing more than rebound romance.

Max swore at his inability to keep his mind on business.

He and Scout had discussed their love lives while they were baring their souls. He hadn't been in a serious relationship in years; she had just broken off an engagement to a friend of her father's. A guy her father had trained for special forces during his last year in the military. Gage had since left the service and was working in private security. He and Scout's father had run into each other just weeks before his death. She'd said that Gage had been there for her just as her uncle had. A few months later he'd asked her to marry him.

Max poured the milk and exiled thoughts of Gage from his mind. Scout was not Max's girlfriend. They'd had sex, that's all. And now she was in trouble. He would do what he could to help her while still doing his job...nothing more. Her current or past love life had nothing to do with anything.

Gritting his teeth, he sauntered back into the living room and plopped the glass of milk down before her. "There you go," he muttered.

She looked up at him, obviously startled by his tone. "Am I missing something?"

Max seated himself directly across from her. "We should talk about business now," he said.

She shrugged. "Fine." She took a bite of her sandwich, her mouth barely fitting around it, then moaned appreciatively as she chewed. After she swallowed, she licked her lips as if unwilling to miss even the most minute morsel.

Max almost choked on his beer. How could anyone make eating look that sensual?

She smiled then. "You remembered that I like mustard."

Yes, he remembered. What did that say about him? That he was hung up on her? He forced down a bite of sandwich. No. He was not hung up on her. He just didn't like guys named Gage.

"What is it that Alexon thinks you stole from them?" Might as well get to the heart of the matter. Alexon had hired him to find her and bring her in because she had something that belonged to them. They had failed to provide the details concerning the absconded item, and he couldn't do his job to the best of his ability if he was left in the dark.

"Like I said." She swallowed a gulp of milk. "You won't believe me."

Max leaned back in his chair and folded his arms over his chest. He wanted answers. Now. Before his mind wandered back into dangerous territory. "Try me," he insisted again none too gently, more irritated with himself than with her.

She nibbled on a chip, then looked directly into his eyes. "It's me they want. Just me."

The telephone rang, the sound coming from the kitchen. Scout blinked and looked away from his intent stare. She knew she'd startled him—that had been her goal. But it was the truth…basically, anyway.

"Excuse me," he muttered as he pushed back his chair and went to answer the phone.

He disappeared into the kitchen and the telephone stopped midring. She massaged her forehead with the tips of her fingers. How was she going to make her explanation sound credible without giving away the rest of the story? Max was too smart to swallow just any old line. She had to find a way to make him believe her enough that he would willingly go against what he'd been assigned to do.

That might be impossible.

Pierce Maxwell was dedicated to duty. She knew that kind of loyalty all too well. She suffered with the malady. It could be a royal pain when one needed to avoid the truth. She heaved a disgusted sigh and looked at her food. She needed to eat. She'd missed lunch and it was after 9:00 p.m. Nourishment was necessary to her and the baby. With that thought, she picked up her sandwich and took another bite. Somehow she would find a way to work this out. Keeping her baby safe was top priority, but bringing her uncle's killer to justice was very important, as well.

Just then she noticed the cordless phone and base sitting in plain view on a table near the bottom of the stairs.

Why had he gone to the kitchen to answer the phone when one sat only a few feet away?

Scout pushed herself from her chair and walked over to the telephone sitting so innocently on the table. She picked up the handset and looked at the ringer selection. It was turned off. So that explained why she hadn't heard it ring. But why hadn't he used this one? Her finger went automatically to the talk button and she depressed it, then slowly raised the handset to her ear. A dial tone greeted her.

He'd already hung up.

His approaching steps confirmed her fears.

She quickly replaced the handset and hurried back to the dining table.

He entered the room just as she resumed her seat. She smiled stiffly.

With the carton of milk in one hand and a couple of snack cakes in the other, he said, "More milk?" He tossed the cakes on the table. "It's the best dessert I can come up with on short notice."

Guilt was written all over his face. He was hiding something from her. She shook her head in answer to his milk question. Were Alexon's men on the way here right now? Would Max allow them to take her away if she begged him to help her? Could she risk telling him the whole truth?

"I'm afraid they'll kill me when they're through with me," she said quietly, her gaze locked with his.

Max set the carton down, then took his seat across from her, his expression carefully controlled. "Why would they do that, Scout? I can't go on guesswork. I need some answers here. I can't help you without answers."

It took every ounce of control she possessed not to get up and run like hell. She wanted to trust Max...but what had that call been about?

"Who phoned?" She hadn't realized she was going to ask the question until the words were out of her mouth. She hardened her gaze, allowing him to see the distrust she felt in spite of her desire not to.

Most people probably wouldn't have even noticed his hesitation, it was so slight. But she did.

"Douglas Cooper. He's with the Colby Agency, as well."

She remembered the name. Cooper was the guy who had picked up Max after Alexon released them four months ago. Cooper wasn't exactly the kind of guy a woman forgot. Tall, dark and handsome was a cliché, but it was the best description of the man. His charm came as automatically as breathing. She knew that kind of polish and charm. Cooper came from money. Big money. Old money. It didn't take an investigator's eye to see that.

"I remember him. What did he want?"

Max almost laughed at the question. She wasn't going to let her guard down easily. She didn't trust him enough right now. Whatever had happened in the past four months, she was as skittish as a skater on thin ice.

There was no point lying and raising her suspicions even higher. She, apparently, read him more easily than he would have liked. Few people had ever been able to do that. That she could spoke volumes about the time they'd spent together. She'd watched him more closely than he'd realized, getting to know him in the same way he had her. "He asked if I had you in custody yet," he said bluntly.

Though she hadn't been moving prior to his frank statement, a stillness claimed her now that went far deeper than the physical.

"And what did you tell him?" Her tone was cool, but carefully controlled.

"I told him yes."

Neither moved or spoke for one tense second that

elapsed into five. The fight-or-flight instinct had grabbed her by the throat. He could see it in her eyes. She was ready to cut her losses and run. But something—some infinitesimal something—kept her still awhile longer.

''They'll kill me,'' she said finally, her voice eerily calm and as cool as a breeze blowing straight in from the Arctic. ''Eventually. There won't be a choice. I know things…too much to be allowed to live.''

''Why? Just tell me why so I can help you.'' He wanted to lean forward. To place his hand over the one of hers poised on the edge of the table, ready to push her away and facilitate her escape. Instead, he remained motionless for fear of setting off the wrong chain of events. She was visibly fragile right now. He didn't want her to feel any more vulnerable than she already was. She wanted to come off as tough and she did, on the surface. But he could see her resolve crumbling from the inside out.

''The virus.'' She blinked, started to look away but changed her mind at the last second, forcing her gaze back to his. ''K-141. I carry the secret to the antidote. They want it. Want me. Regardless of the price.''

His instincts prickled, rousing him to an even higher state of alert. ''Why just you? Why not me, too? We're both immune. That doesn't make sense.''

She did look away then. Max swore softly. She was lying. At least about part of it.

''I can't answer that.'' She pushed her chair back and stood. ''I only know that my uncle gave his life trying to protect me.''

Max stood in turn, matching her wary stance. "I'll confront Alexon. Demand to know why they want you. And I'll keep you safe until I find the truth." He inclined his head and searched her suspicious gaze. "If you'll let me."

"You swear?" she pressed. Her tone had gone from icy to hot. "I can trust you? You won't give me up to Alexon?"

"I swear."

Something changed in her eyes then. And Max was certain for the first time since he'd tackled her in that cemetery that she finally believed him.

She started to say more, but the sound of someone pounding on the front door cut her off.

The racket came again, this time louder, and hard enough to rattle the door on its hinges. "Open up! We know you're in there, Miss Jackson!"

"They're here." Her frightened gaze swung back to meet his. The words were barely more than a breath of sound. "You lied to me."

Chapter Five

"Come with me." Max reached for Scout, those blue eyes beseeching her to trust him, one long-fingered hand extended toward her.

But how could she?

Something slammed hard against the front door. Her attention darted in that direction. They were coming in. Another loud crash echoed from the kitchen. The back door was covered, too.

She was trapped.

"Let's go!" Max grabbed her hand and pulled her toward the stairs.

She frowned. If they went upstairs, they'd be trapped.

"Wait!" She dug in her heels.

He shot a look over his shoulder, not bothering to slow down, making her stumble after him. "There's no time."

He was right. If they were going to get out of this, it had to be now.

Right now.

She reassured herself as she flew up the stairs behind him that he must have a plan. Max was too smart to get himself trapped like this.

"Lock the door," he ordered as soon as they'd skidded to a halt in the master bathroom.

"Don't you think we—"

"Lock it!"

She quickly obeyed the roared command. When she whirled back to face him he was climbing out the bathroom window. Her confusion erupted into outright panic then.

What the heck was he doing?

She couldn't go out the window. Her hand went to her stomach as she considered the distance to the ground.

No way.

She couldn't risk injury to the child she carried...but how could she explain that to Max without giving away her secret?

Once fully through the opening, he moved to the right side of the window. "Come on," he urged in a stage whisper.

She stepped closer, peeked out beneath the raised sash. Her eyes widened as she peered downward. He stood on a tiny ledge. The ground was at least twenty feet below.

"Are you nuts?" she demanded, glaring at him, furious now. He'd dragged her up here and now she was trapped. Maybe he could risk serious bodily injury, but she couldn't.

He motioned to the other side of the window. "We can climb down the antenna tower. It's sturdy. Completely safe," he urged.

Her gaze swung to the triangular-shaped, steel tower that soared from the ground upward, extending some ten feet above the roofline. The tower she had no problem with. It was the twelve or so feet

of narrow ledge between the window and the lad-
derlike structure that gave her pause.

She shook her head. "I can't do it." Fear surged
into her throat. Her stomach knotted with apprehension.

"I'll help you. Just get out here," he ordered.
"They'll be in the house and up those stairs any
minute now."

Scout considered the alternative for about two
seconds before scrambling through the opening. It
was a good thing the builder hadn't skimped on the
windows in this house, she thought, panic hovering
just under the surface of her flimsy grip on control.
Some bathroom windows were far too small for a
child to climb through, much less an adult.

Inordinately thankful for the large sash, she an-
gled her body awkwardly, reaching downward with
her foot until her toe touched the narrow ledge.
Holding her breath, she eased out fully, bracing both
feet in a classic ballet second position on the ledge.
The fingers of her left hand gripped the edge of the
window casing as she simultaneously flattened herself against the exterior wall. Her heart thundered so
hard she could scarcely draw a breath. Over and
over she told herself that she was okay, she wouldn't
fall. All she had to do now was move....

Every muscle in her body froze.

"I've got you," Max murmured, easing closer
and grabbing hold of her arm. "Just scoot toward
the tower."

She swallowed hard, told herself she could do it.
One second stretched into five before she persuaded
her traitorous body to respond to the command.
Slowly, one pulse-pounding inch at a time, she

forced herself to move toward the tower. As soon as he had cleared the window, Max pulled down the sash. Weakness washed over her, making her knees want to buckle. She was still too far away to reach the tower. The window was closed. If she fell…

"Just a little farther and you can reach out and grab on," Max urged. "I won't let you fall."

She wanted to glare at him and tell him what she thought of his escape route, but she didn't dare make any sudden moves. There was nothing to hold on to, nothing to keep her plastered against that wall except absolute stillness and sheer force of will.

She had no intention of moving again.

"They're coming," Max urged. "Please, Scout, trust me. I won't let you fall."

Fear burned through her veins. He was right. She could hear the stampede of boots on the stairs. What good would it do her to protect her child from one threat only to fall victim to another?

They had to get out of here.

Holding her breath and keeping her gaze fixed on the tower, she inched toward it.

"Reach out and grab a rung," Max told her. "I've got you." He held on tight to her left arm.

Scout extended her right arm, straining, reaching. Her heart stilled in her chest as she stretched the last required fraction of an inch. Max held her tightly in his strong grip. Her fingers latched onto the cool metal. The breath she'd been holding hissed from her lungs. Her fingers curled around the steel, then she swung a foot onto a lower rung. Before she allowed herself time to fully consider the danger, she had climbed halfway to the ground. Max followed closely.

When they were both safely on the ground, he ushered her toward the front of the house, careful to stay within the shadows of the trees. He withdrew the keys to his SUV and dangled them for her to see. She smiled. Good old Max. He was always prepared. Seconds later they climbed into the vehicle they'd exited not so long ago.

The roar of the engine alerted those inside the cabin. A cacophony of voices erupted as bodies spilled out onto the deck. Max shoved the gearshift into Reverse and floored the accelerator. Scout powered down the window and laid some ground fire to hold off any attempts to follow.

A 180-degree turn later and they were speeding down the narrow winding road that led from Max's cabin to Crystal Lake proper. While he pushed the SUV for all it was worth to put more asphalt behind them, Scout kept watch for any pursuers.

She swore as two pairs of headlights bobbed over the hill some hundred yards back. ''Here they come.''

''Buckle up,'' Max ordered.

Though she followed his direction, her mind went abruptly to a whole other line of thinking. ''How did they find me?'' she demanded, suspicion making her tone harsh. Though she had to admit she doubted Max would be whisking her away if he intended for those guys to get their hands on her, still, someone had to have tipped them off.

''I don't know,'' Max said flatly, his attention never leaving the highway.

''If it wasn't you, then it must have been your pal Cooper.'' She twisted around in her seat long enough to notice that the tails were steadily gaining on them.

"They couldn't have known where I would take you," Max said, more to himself than to her. He glanced at her then. "And Cooper wouldn't have given out the information without my authorization."

Scout shrugged. "Well, maybe those guys are psychic." She was just about sick of deception. If Max was playing a game with her—

"Hold on," he warned a split second before taking a hard right.

Bracing herself, Scout craned her neck to look behind them once more. The next vehicle skidded with the effort, but made the turn.

"I could take out one of their tires," she suggested, already reaching to release the confining seat belt. She'd need to be in the back seat. The second vehicle almost wiped out on the turn, but managed to straighten up and rocket toward them.

"No!"

His tone startled her. "Why the hell not?" she snapped back. "Are those guys friends of yours?" Her pulse rate had already picked up an extra twenty beats per minute. How was she supposed to trust him, considering all the mixed signals he appeared to be giving?

"We're not shooting unless they shoot first. If those are Alexon's men—"

"If?" Scout made a scoffing sound. "Did you believe nothing I told you? Alexon is the enemy. How do I get that through your thick skull?"

"What's this?" Max shifted his attention from the road to the rearview mirror and back.

A third vehicle, yet another SUV, was attempting to pass the two already in pursuit of them. Scout didn't even want to know how fast the vehicle they were in was traveling. The tingling in the bottom of her feet was indication enough that it was far faster than she preferred. The realization that the enemy was swiftly overtaking their position only made matters worse.

"Hold on," Max cautioned before taking another sudden turn.

Tires squealed and this time Scout was certain the SUV would topple over...but somehow it didn't.

More screaming tires screeched behind them. She looked back just in time to see the third SUV, the one that had passed the others, slide to a stop across the road, effectively blocking the path of their original pursuers.

Frowning, Scout kept an eye on the situation until the vehicles were out of sight. "I don't get it." She shook her head and faced forward once more. "Who was that?"

Max didn't let up, obviously determined to put as much distance as possible between the other vehicles and theirs. "It couldn't have been Cooper, and no one else from the agency knows where we are at the moment."

"How do you know it wasn't your friend Cooper? It wasn't like we could make out the color or model of the vehicle. We certainly couldn't see the driver. Does he drive something other than an SUV?" Didn't all the macho types go for the muscle vehicles?

Max exhaled loudly. "What he drives is beside the point. I know it wasn't Cooper because he's in

Houston, probably keeping your assistant company about now.''

Every time Scout thought he couldn't do or say anything else to throw her off balance, he proved her wrong. ''You thought you could get to me through my assistant?''

He shrugged. ''I had to have a backup plan in case you didn't show at the cemetery.''

She shook her head. He thought entirely too much like her.

''Now what?'' she asked archly.

''We find someplace else to crash for a few hours. We both need some sleep and we need to talk some more. There are a few things we need to get straight.'' He still hadn't let up on the gas. The landscape whizzed by in a blur of black and dark green. ''But first we've got to stash this SUV and find alternate transportation.''

''This time I choose the location,'' she insisted. ''I'm not comfortable with your choices.''

Max laughed. The sound held little humor, but it helped ease the tension. For the moment, she had to assume that he was on her side. But the instant she got the slightest inkling otherwise, she was out of here.

Forty-five minutes later, Max had gotten lost in the downtown Chicago traffic. He had decided that someone from Alexon had followed him from the cemetery to his place at Crystal Lake. That was the only feasible explanation. Apparently, whomever it was had gotten a little trigger happy and tried to horn in on Max's territory. Max had made it clear to Alexon before taking this assignment that he would bring Scout in on his own terms. Alexon had agreed to that condition. What they didn't need to know was that Max wanted to learn Scout's side of things before he took any drastic measures. Something about all this didn't feel right. He had to know why.

The third vehicle must have been from Alexon as well, since no one else had even known he would be waiting for Scout at the cemetery. Maybe Alexon had sent a team to put a stop to the loose cannons who'd forced Max and Scout into fleeing. He was rationalizing, he knew. Something just didn't add up.

A quick call to Victoria was all it would take to get Alexon off his back…if they were the culprits.

They had to be, of course. No one else had been privy to his immediate plans.

Max parked in the space he used every day when he came to the office. The agency kept two nondescript sedans and an SUV for just this sort of situation.

"Where are we?" Scout demanded, but she didn't hesitate to emerge from the SUV when he did.

He gestured toward the upscale skyscraper across the lot. "The Colby Agency. We're picking up that alternate transportation I mentioned to you earlier."

Without responding, she followed him into the building. The night watchman nodded once in greeting after Max showed his ID. When the elevator opened onto the fourth floor, Scout made a little sound of surprise.

"So this is where you work," she commented, her gaze roaming the luxurious reception area. He didn't miss the glimmer of approval in those gray eyes.

"This is it," he replied, leading the way to his own office. During their time in isolation together she'd told him about her office in Houston. He'd even thought about just showing up there one day to see her…to ask why she'd never returned any of his calls. But he hadn't. Instead, he'd forced thoughts of Scout out of his mind and focused on work. It was the safest thing to do, right? Why risk further rejection? She hadn't looked back, so why should he?

Max pushed away the past and focused on the present. He had a job to do. He hesitated at his office door, waiting for Scout to catch up. She lingered, admiring the elegant paintings hung along the main corridor.

"Is anyone else here?" she asked, glancing first at the overhead lights and then scanning the bottoms of the closed doors along the corridor. The offices were all dark.

He stepped into his office and flipped on the light. "It's just us. Security prefers that we leave on the reception area and corridor lights."

She nodded and moved through the open doorway.

Max crossed to his desk. All agents possessed a set of keys to each vehicle owned by the agency. He'd decided on a sedan, something totally different and a bit more anonymous than his SUV. He'd noted that all three vehicles were in the lot when they'd parked.

Scout studied the photographs and framed career acknowledgments on his wall. For reasons he couldn't explain, he felt unexpectedly self-conscious. "I'm usually a little neater than this," he felt compelled to say when her gaze settled on the numerous stacks of papers on his desk.

She only smiled and drifted around the room, analyzing, touching things he'd grown so accustomed to that he rarely noticed their existence anymore. But having her there suddenly made the most inane object seem significant.

She picked up a marksman trophy he'd won years ago in a DEA-sponsored competition. After a moment she moved on to other awards, carefully considering each before going to the next. Forcing a casualness he definitely didn't feel, he checked his voice mail and the In box on his desk. When she moved up behind him, he tensed, instantly aware of her unique scent and the energy she gave off.

''Is this your family?''

He turned to find her holding a framed photograph. The one his sister had insisted they have made last year. She'd complained that the Maxwells hadn't had a family portrait done in half a lifetime. So Max, his younger brother, older sister and Mom and Dad had all gotten together for a sitting. Max had to admit he was pretty damn proud of his family. His sister had been right about the need to have the photograph done. None of them was getting any younger.

''Yeah, that's the Maxwell clan.'' He eased down onto the edge of his desk and watched her face as she studied the picture.

''Nice.''

He tapped the frame next to his brother's image. ''That's Derrick. He's in the Air Force, stationed in Alaska right now.'' Max realized for the first time that he hadn't seen his brother since this portrait was made. Damn, time flew quickly. ''That's Fiona. She's the oldest and the bossiest.'' His sister always engineered the family get-togethers. She was the most organized. Everything a guy could want in a big sister. ''Mom and Dad, of course,'' he added, briefly touching the glass above their beloved faces.

''I don't remember my mom,'' Scout said softly, the words scarcely a whisper. ''I know her face from photographs and I can vaguely remember her voice.'' She looked at Max then, a sadness she either couldn't or didn't attempt to hide in her eyes. ''She used to sing me a lullaby every night. I can remember that....'' She shrugged. ''Not much else, though.''

The full ramifications of Scout's situation hit Max then. She had not only lost her mother, but her father was gone, as well. She had no siblings. The man she called Uncle, the only family she had left, had just been murdered. She was even accused by some of being involved on some level. Max couldn't imagine how awful that must feel.

''I'm sorry.'' As soon as the words were out of his mouth, he regretted having said them. Her expression hardened in a heartbeat.

''Don't be. Life isn't always fair. I got over it.''

She set the photograph of his family back in its place of honor on his credenza, and skirted his desk. Careful to keep her back turned to him, she folded her arms protectively over her middle. Max closed his eyes and chastised himself for being so thoughtless. She'd simply asked if the people were his family, not for a dossier on each.

He retrieved the keys to the gray sedan from his middle desk drawer and pumped some lightness into his tone when he inquired, "So, where are we going now?"

She swiveled to face him, all that silky dark hair swinging around her shoulders with the move, her expression one of confusion. "What?"

"You said you were going to choose the place, right?" He tamped down the urge to smile. She hadn't believed he would go along with her demand without an argument. But he needed her trust. He'd play it her way as long as her decision didn't put her in any additional danger.

Her confusion melted into surprise. "Right." She moved toward the door, her arms still folded firmly. "We have to make a stop first," she said, pausing in the corridor outside his open door.

He clicked off the overhead light and pulled the door shut behind him. "What kind of stop?"

"I need the things I brought with me from Houston," she clarified. "The motel's not far from here."

Alexon hadn't been able to track her down. They were convinced she hadn't taken public transportation from Houston. No tickets had been purchased in her name, nor in any of the aliases she'd been known to use in her business. But then, that didn't mean she hadn't made reservations in a name no one knew about. Fake ID was as easy to pick up as gasoline at a service station. Certainly Alexon couldn't flash a photo and question every employee at the airports, train and bus stations. And there was always the possibility that she'd simply rented a car and driven the entire distance.

"You didn't mention how you got here," he

noted aloud as they boarded the elevator in the reception area once more.

She smiled at him. "No. I didn't."

THE MOTEL LAY on the outskirts of town and epitomized the term "seedy." It irritated Max that she would stay in a dump like this, where most of the tenants rented by the hour versus by the night. Did she have no concept of personal safety?

What was he thinking? This was the same woman who'd gone into a South American jungle after a lost scientist. She was fearless.

"Nice place," he said dryly as he entered the shabby room behind her.

"It served its purpose," she retorted, just as cynically.

She tossed a duffel onto the bed, unzipped it and immediately started to stuff her personal belongings into it. He watched as toothbrush, toothpaste and simple cosmetics landed on top of clothing she'd never unpacked.

He was impressed with her ability to travel light. Most women, in his experience, would be lost without a blow dryer, curling iron and a dozen other "essential" items. Scout carried none of those things. Just the basics, nothing more. And, of course, her weapon.

When she'd completed her work, everything she'd brought on the trip fit nicely into the one duffel. Now he was really impressed.

Just when he'd decided that Scout was seriously different from the other women he'd known, she picked up what looked like a purse. A very large purse.

He sighed. The concept had been too good to be true, he admitted.

As if reading his mind, she shrugged the shoulder now bearing the weight of the gigantic pocketbook. "My home office," she explained.

It was his turn to be confused. "Home office?"

She opened the huge bag and showed him that it contained file folders, a mass of papers, a cellular phone and what looked like a laptop. Not a hairbrush or compact in sight. There was a small wallet/coin purse combination, he noticed. But that one item appeared to be her only concession to feminine necessity.

"Everything I know about Alexon is in here," she said solemnly. "I'm trusting you with all I have. I hope you're not going to let me down, Max."

He held her gaze for one tense beat before answering. Somehow he had to convince her that she could trust him completely. "I won't let you down."

She nodded and released a heavy breath. "We'll see."

"So," he said offhandedly, "where are we going from here?"

"My uncle's place," she said succinctly.

Her *dead* uncle's place?

Before he could question her reasoning, she added, "No one will think to look for us there. We'll be safe…at least for a little while."

An emotion in her eyes that he couldn't quite define reaffirmed her words. *Safe* was all that mattered at the moment.

Chapter Six

Harold Atkins's house sat on a corner lot in a small, quiet residential area in the suburbs of Chicago. Made of stone and reminiscent of nineteenth century cottage style, the small home was surrounded by lush landscaping and towering trees. Weeping willows swayed each time the night air stirred. A corner streetlight lit the small, meticulously maintained front yard a little too well, ensuring the necessity for a rear entry.

"Besides the obvious that this is the least likely place anyone will look," Max began, breaking the long silence, "why are we here?"

He knew she had a reason. Scout wasn't afraid of anything. Well, except maybe heights, he amended, remembering the climb out of his house. Not only had she gone into that jungle to rescue a missing scientist, she'd come back to help him, knowing there was a good possibility he was in enemy hands. That knowledge had not stopped her from coming back to face whatever stood in her way. Breaking into a murdered man's house couldn't just be about staying safe. There had to be more to it. She simply wasn't stating her reasons yet.

"He always kept a spare key hidden around back," she said, choosing to ignore Max's question. "Circle the block again and park on that side of the street, maybe a few houses down."

"You're the boss," Max said. Admittedly, he would have used the same strategy had the place been his choice. Still, it irked him that she continued to behave so distrustfully. His only shortcoming was that Alexon had hired him. What could have happened between her and Alexon these past four months to cause this sort of intense distrust? And he couldn't even begin to fathom how Alexon could think she'd had anything to do with her uncle's murder. Then again, what did Max really know about her that she hadn't told him?

He swallowed tightly as he parked the car three houses away from Atkins's residence. He knew very little about her other than the intelligence facts the agency had uncovered, the stories she'd told him and every square inch of her body.

His own body tensed at the memories that immediately flooded his mind. He couldn't be that wrong about her. Whatever was going on, she wasn't the bad guy.

Somehow he had to help her sort out the situation.

Keeping to the shadows of the tree-lined walk and then to those cast by the copse of trees delineating the border between the Atkins yard and his closest neighbor's, Max and Scout made their way to the back of the cottage. Within seconds they were inside.

"Help me close all the blinds and pull the drapes. That way we can turn on at least a few lights."

Avoiding small pieces of furniture and plants

proved virtually impossible as he moved through the darkness. Scout, being familiar with the interior, fared better. Eventually they accomplished their goal and turned on a couple of lights—the one over the stove in the kitchen, the wall sconces in the hallway and the desk lamp in her uncle's home office.

To his surprise, she brought up the subject of food. "I'm starved," she muttered as she headed toward the refrigerator. Giving her grace, their dinner had been interrupted. He could eat as well.

If being in her recently deceased uncle's house bothered her in any way, Max hadn't picked up on it yet. That puzzled him. If the man was like family, she should be feeling some sort of strong emotion just being here. Or maybe she was good at hiding her feelings. Too early to tell, he decided, giving her the benefit of the doubt once more.

Max knew he was rationalizing far too much in this investigation. He was personally involved and that wasn't good, but he couldn't change it. He wasn't even sure he wanted to. The time they'd spent together had touched him far deeper than even he wanted to admit.

They dined on ham sandwiches, chips and iced tea. Neither spoke as the meal was consumed. Max wanted to ask her more questions, but instinctively knew that she didn't want to discuss the matter at the moment. Her expression was so closed that he could feel her withdrawal. Had he failed so miserably to get his point across? Yes, Alexon had hired him, but he was on her side. Without her trust he would never have her half of the story.

"I know you don't want to believe me," she said suddenly, the sound of her voice startling him from his worrisome thoughts. "But I'm telling the truth about Alexon. And, just so you know, I rented a car under an alias and drove here."

His gaze connected with hers across the expanse of Formica. He'd figured as much. The weapon she carried made a commercial flight less than attractive. "Why don't you start from the beginning and tell me what happened?"

She touched the paper napkin to her lips, then set it aside. "The trouble started about a month after we were released."

Max tossed his own napkin onto his empty plate and relaxed more fully into his chair, giving her his undivided attention.

"Alexon kept calling me back in for further tests." She shrugged. "It was really ridiculous. They'd call me up and say a plane ticket was waiting for me at the airline counter, and that they'd like me to come the very next day. Finally, when I'd had enough of jetting back and forth between Houston and Chicago, I flatly refused."

She fell silent for a long moment as she studied the faux wood grain of the tabletop. "That was about two months ago. Two of their henchmen showed up at my door one evening and said that I had to come back to Chicago with them because my uncle needed me."

Max frowned. "And you're sure these two were from Alexon?"

She nodded. "That's where they took me as soon as we arrived in Chicago."

Allowing that information to soak in, he waited for her to continue.

"They held me prisoner for six weeks."

The announcement stunned him. "What?"

"Alexon—" she smiled, and it was not pleasant "—to put it in their own words, 'detained me' for six weeks."

"Like before? In isolation?"

She nodded. "Just like before. Only this time I was alone."

Scout could plainly see the impact her words had on him: disbelief, outrage, then more disbelief. He wanted to believe her, but his rational side kept intruding. She had to tread carefully here. She wanted to come clean with him, but she still couldn't trust him with the entire truth. Not yet. No matter how badly she wanted to. The safety of her baby was top priority. Max hadn't earned that much of her trust yet. She prayed with all her heart that he wouldn't let her down.

He visibly grappled to regain his control, and when he had, he demanded, "Was there some compelling reason for this incarceration? Did they suspect you were coming down with the virus, after all?"

Like the good investigator he was, he wanted to find a reasonable, rational explanation for Alexon's actions. What he didn't know and she couldn't prove was that it was greed, pure and simple. They wanted the antidote that badly. The financial opportunities were boundless.

"No. It wasn't anything like that." She shifted in her chair, nearly too exhausted to think. But they had to have this talk. He had to understand what she was up against. "They think I'm the key to the elusive antidote they've been trying to come up with. They want to study me..." She swallowed back the emotion clogging her throat. "To take things from me." She blinked back the tears that immediately filled her eyes. "It's the only way to correct Kirstenof's antidote."

Shaking his head, Max pushed away from the table and started to pace the small kitchen. "This doesn't make sense." He stopped long enough to stare at her. "We were both immune. Why just you? Why didn't they come after me?"

Now came the tricky part. She moistened her lips and squared her shoulders. "I think it's because I don't have any real family or close friends." She shrugged, suddenly self-conscious. "I'm kind of a loner. After Uncle Harold moved here, we didn't see each other often and I focused on my work. Anyway, I think they feel comfortable taking advantage of me, since there's no one to raise a fuss about my absence." Her gaze locked with his then. She hadn't meant to look directly at him, but she couldn't help herself. "No one would care if I suddenly came up missing. My assistant would simply think I'd gone out on a case and didn't come back. That happens to private investigators quite often, you know."

She could see the tension escalating in him. His posture grew more rigid, his jaw set more firmly, those incredible lips thinned into a grim line. He was upset at how she'd been treated. Maybe he cared more than she'd thought. She sighed, weary of her own foolish hopes. She didn't want to make too much of his reaction. They'd had sex...nothing more.

But it had felt like so much more to her.

His pacing stopped and his eyes bored straight into hers. "Did they hurt you in any way?"

She had to stiffen her spine to stop the trembling. She wanted so much to be held in his strong arms. To believe for just one minute that he really cared. That *someone* actually cared. "Lots of samples. Blood, urine, the usual."

He didn't need to know about the sonograms. She'd lain on that examination table and cried, fearing for her unborn child's life. But no one had cared. She'd been a prisoner with no rights. None.

"What did your uncle say about this?" The harsh words grated across her already raw nerve endings. "Where the hell was he all this time? He worked for Alexon, for God's sake."

Emotion welled inside her. She struggled to remain calm on the surface. She had to keep this on a professional level. Couldn't risk things getting personal this time. As much as she wanted to lean on Max the man, she needed Max the protector and investigator more.

"For the first four weeks of my forced stay at the facility, Harold wasn't aware of what had happened. He only knew that I hadn't returned his calls. Alexon forced me to phone my assistant and tell her that my latest case required a deep-cover stint and not to expect to hear from me for a few weeks. But then Harold found out." If she called him Harold, kept her focus on his position as head of Alexon's security, maybe she could keep the emotions at bay a few more minutes.

Max turned his chair around, sat astride it and braced his arms on the back. "What did he do?" His words were tight, clipped. He was angry.

Or maybe his more rational side had kicked in and he didn't believe her. She closed her eyes and drew in a deep, fortifying breath. She had to get through this without breaking down.

"He engineered my escape."

Once again she'd shocked Max. He definitely hadn't expected her to say that.

"That's why they killed him," she added when Max asked no questions. "I've been hiding out since."

He shook his head in disbelief, confusion etched across his handsome face. "This whole antidote thing is the reason?" His tone reaffirmed her suspicions that he couldn't quite grasp the story.

"Yes. I know you don't want to believe it, but it's the truth. Harold—" she swallowed convulsively "—had discovered some disturbing information. That's how he put two and two together and realized I wasn't simply out on a case, that I'd been abducted. Whatever he found, it's the key to why they're after me."

"He didn't tell you any specifics about this information?" More incredulity. Max didn't believe her. That was clear.

"He told me he didn't have all the facts yet, but that he wanted me safe until he got to the bottom of the matter." At Max's continued look of skepticism, she added, "He said he was putting together a file. I'm guessing that it's here somewhere."

"So that's why you wanted to come here?"

"Partly." She didn't say that she was here mainly to be near her uncle's things. To close her eyes and draw in the scent of his home, of his life. God, she missed him!

"And you're certain that it was Alexon's men who killed him?"

''Man,'' she corrected. ''There were four of them, but only one did the killing.'' She fell silent a moment as she battled for composure. Flashes of memory darted through her mind—the struggle, the sound of that lethal shot. She blinked furiously, but it was no use. Tears spilled past her lashes. She wiped her eyes and stood abruptly. ''I need to start looking for the file. You can help if you want.''

Max watched her walk away, the need to take her into his arms and comfort her very nearly overpowering. But she didn't want that from him right now. He could sense the emotional distance she struggled to maintain. The last thing either of them needed was for things to get personal again. They were far too personal already.

The story she'd just told him unsettled him as nothing else ever had. The Colby Agency had done business with Alexon for years. Their reputation was unrivaled in the medical research world. Only Ballard Pharmaceuticals ranked as close to the top. But Max was no fool. A sparkling reputation didn't always mean that a corporation didn't have skeletons in its closets. In some cases, holding top spot was not accomplished without moral—and legal—compromises. He couldn't imagine why Scout would fabricate such an outrageous story.

Though he had been hired by Alexon, he would do the right thing. And the right thing was to get to the bottom of this mystery. Alexon might not like his tactics, but they had agreed to his condition. He intended to see that they stuck by their word. If Scout thought her uncle had a file on Alexon's wrongdoing, Max would do everything he could to help her find it. He would keep an open mind until he had reason to believe something one way or the other. When he contacted Alexon again he would demand to know why their people were following him.

Deciding to start with the kitchen, Max opened door after door, drawer after drawer. He systematically perused the contents of each before moving on. Carefully opening canisters and plastic containers, he insured that Harold hadn't hidden anything where he thought no one would look. Then Max checked the fridge and freezer. Still nothing.

He heard Scout moving around in the office, which he had expected, so he took the living room. Comfortable and cluttered, the room offered numerous places to hide documents. He methodically inspected each piece of furniture and every single nook and cranny. His final step was to remove photographs from picture frames.

All along the mantel stood frame after frame. Almost all displayed photographs of Scout at various ages in her life. Max took his time, studying the images. Scout as a child, a teenager, and then a woman...

He smiled as he fingered the smiling face of the little girl grasping the hand of what must be her father. The same gray eyes stared back from him, and they both had raven hair. Her father wore a military uniform, and Max remembered that he'd been in special forces or some other elite, covert unit. He'd spent a lot of time away from home, leaving Scout to be cared for by her faux uncle, Harold Atkins. Judging by the sheer number of photographs, Max guessed Harold had thought of Scout as a daughter. No question there.

There was one picture of Scout and her mother. Or at least Max thought it was her mother. Scout was just a toddler, the woman a dark-haired beauty. The shape of her face reminded Max of Scout. Yes, it had to be her mother. He remembered that Scout had said she'd died from complications resulting from an emergency appendectomy. Her father had been stationed in some tiny village in a third world country, and proper medical care had come too late.

Max's gaze returned to the man holding his daughter's hand. He wondered if guilt had weighed heavily on those broad shoulders. Had he felt responsible for his wife's death? Had his career been so important that he would drag his wife and small child to such a primitive place?

Max set the framed photograph down and shoved aside that thought. He'd always put career first himself. Who was he to judge what another man had done? Max doubted he would do any better.

He almost laughed out loud then. What was he thinking? He hadn't even taken the time for a wife, much less a family. At thirty-three, and with his career the only constant in his life, he certainly had no right to judge anyone else.

The rest of the photographs told the story of who Olivia Scout Jackson was. She'd loved horseback riding. She rarely wore anything but jeans and T-shirts. She'd told Max how she loved mountain climbing and skating on the edge of danger. His smile died on his lips when he considered that she appeared to be teetering very close to danger right now. Then he frowned. If she loved mountain climbing why had she been afraid to climb down from the second story of his house? He shook his head.

As soon as one detail cleared in his mind, something else jumped in to blur the facts.

There had to be at least some truth to her story. Alexon would not have sent men to check up on Max and her if they weren't desperate to get her back. And if they were that convinced that she had somehow been involved with her uncle's murder, the police as well would be looking for her by now. Still, it simply didn't add up. If the antidote was the motivation, why not come after Max, too? He had the same immunity she did.

It didn't make sense. There had to be more.

After replacing each photograph in its frame, he decided to question her further. The answers she'd given him so far weren't sufficient. He had an uneasy feeling in the pit of his stomach that she was holding something back.

When he entered the strangely quiet home office he found Scout asleep on the small, well-worn sofa. A stack of files sat beside her, one open in her lap, while yet another lay on the floor where it had fallen from her hands.

He moved next to her and crouched down to pick up the wayward pages. That she didn't rouse at his nearness spoke volumes about just how exhausted she really was. He ached to comfort her…to somehow make all this right for her. But he had to know all the facts first.

Two bedrooms and one bathroom were right down the hall. She needed a good night's rest. Before he could talk himself out of it, he'd lifted her in his arms and against his chest. Her eyelids fluttered open and she tensed instantly.

"Shh," he ordered. "You need to sleep. I'm only taking you to bed."

The look of fear or uncertainty on her face made his chest constrict. Did she think he would take advantage of a vulnerable moment like this?

"Don't worry, I'll be taking the couch," he clarified. "I want to be close to the two entry doors."

She relaxed then and made no move to free herself from his grasp. Was she finally beginning to trust him? He hoped so. Taking care not to hold her too tightly, as he so wanted to, he started through the door of the first bedroom he came to.

"Not here." She shook her head, her eyes too bright. "The guest room."

He realized his mistake then. He'd almost taken her into her uncle's room.

When he'd deposited her on her feet next to the guest bed, he drew back the covers and gestured for her to climb beneath them. "Rest. Don't worry about anything. I'll be watching your back. I'm sure we'll find that file."

For one long moment she simply stood there staring up at him. Finally she spoke. "Max, I know you don't really believe me, but you will. When I find that file you'll know the truth."

He balled his hands into fists to keep himself from reaching out and touching her once more. "I do believe that something isn't right here. Alexon hasn't been on the up and up with me and that makes me suspicious of their motivation. But I need solid evidence. I can't go back to Victoria with speculation. I have to have facts."

Scout nodded, her expression strained at best.

"Victoria knows that we were involved on a personal level. It's going to be doubly hard to make this case with that past hanging over our heads.''

"I know." She reached out to him then. The feel of her small hand against his chest, even through the cotton of his shirt, made him tremble inside. "That's why we have to be sure we don't let that happen this time."

She was right. If they weren't careful no one would put any stock in anything they came up with.

"We'll keep things strictly business this time," he agreed. "I don't usually make the same mistake twice." He stared down at her hand and ached to fold his around it. "You have to admit," he added, his gaze going back to hers, "that we did have a hell of a motive. We thought we were going to die."

She drew her hand away and nodded jerkily. "Good night, Max."

Turning, she climbed into the bed, then pulled the covers snugly around her.

"Good night." He felt the need to say more…but what was left? They'd agreed that anything personal would be a mistake. There was nothing else to discuss about the case at the moment. He exhaled a frustrated breath and switched off the light as he left the room. His own emotions were far too close to the surface right now to deal with what was going on with hers. The signals she gave off were so mixed he existed in a perpetual state of confusion.

They needed some distance and a good night's sleep. Things would be clearer in the morning. He was sure of it.

For long minutes after Max walked out of the room Scout lay there unmoving, scarcely breathing. Something inside her threatened to shatter like glass.

She wanted to cry, but she knew if she started it would quickly become uncontrollable. And he would hear. She couldn't do that.

I don't usually make the same mistake twice.

His words knifed through her. He considered their time together to be a mistake.

A mistake.

The realization hurt more than she had believed possible. The pain even cut through her grief for her uncle. She wouldn't have thought anything could rival that hurt, but it did. She felt betrayed, felt as if her heart were being torn from her chest.

She burrowed deeper under the covers and tried hard not to let the tears escape. How could it hurt this much?

And suddenly she knew.

It wasn't about her.

It was about the baby.

His baby.

If he felt the time they'd shared had been a mistake, what would he consider the child they had created?

A mistake.

MAX RECLINED ON THE SOFA in the cluttered living room, forcing his body to relax. He'd turned out all the lights and ensured that all doors and windows were secured. Again he fought the urge to go back to her room, to somehow show her that she meant more to him than simply a case. That they had shared something special during those few days in isolation. But that would be a bad move.

The only way he could help her was to keep his head on straight here.

He needed evidence of her accusations and he had to know that she was telling him all there was to tell. He had to believe that she wasn't holding anything back. And right now he was certain she hadn't come completely clean with him.

She needed to grieve, but that would make her vulnerable. If she allowed that concession, she might just open up. But she might not do that with him close by.

A sound jerked him from his troubled musings.

He listened intently, straining to identify the source.

And then he knew.

Scout was crying…no, sobbing.

He fought the urge to go to her.

He had to keep his distance or risk losing all perspective.

Her life depended on his making the right decisions.

Forcing his eyes to close, he did the only thing he could. He silently endured the pain and suffering…hers and his own.

Chapter Seven

The dream woke her from a restless sleep. Scout sat up in bed, perspiration beading on her skin, her heart pounding in her chest. It was always the same. She walked into the house to find her father dying on the living room floor. She'd tried to help...but it had been too late. God, she hated that dream. Why, after all this time, didn't it just go away? She didn't want to think about it, much less recall the moment so vividly. As her respiration returned to normal, another fist of panic broadsided her.

Where was she?

She blinked.

Forced her eyes to adjust to the darkness.

Her uncle's house.

He was dead.

Pain stabbed her deep in the heart.

She pressed her hand to her abdomen. But she still had her baby. No one would take her child from her.

Max.

He was here. She drew her knees up to her chest and hugged them. He still didn't believe her—not completely, anyway. She could sense that he knew she was holding something back.

A mistake.

Tears burned in her eyes once more. Eyes that were already puffy from crying herself to sleep. It was the first time she'd cried since her father died.

She shoved the covers back and got out of the bed. He hadn't simply died. Someone had murdered him, just as her uncle had been murdered. Only this time she could identify the murderer. She knew his voice. And she would not rest until she brought him to justice.

That effort would also help her bring Alexon down. After all, it was one of Alexon's men who'd killed her uncle.

While she'd allowed herself to be vulnerable and cry for her latest losses, that of her beloved uncle and the father of her child, she'd come to one glaringly final conclusion: she did not need Pierce Maxwell. She could do this on her own. That's how she'd started out and how she intended to finish. She hadn't asked for his interference. In fact, the very enemy she sought to bring to its knees had hired him. And now that she knew his true feelings, she had no reason to trust him.

None whatsoever.

The past was, as he'd so eloquently put it, a mistake.

She would live with that.

She'd harbored no illusions of white picket fences or happily ever afters.

Now all she had to do was give him the slip.

Easier said than done, most likely.

There was the file, in any case. She needed to find

the file her uncle had put together on the enemy—
Alexon. She'd thoroughly searched his office, saving
the file drawers, the most obvious storage place, for
last. She'd come up empty-handed. Max had
searched the kitchen and living room and come up
with nothing. That left only the bedrooms and bathroom, which she would have checked earlier had she
not fallen asleep.

There was no time like the present, she decided.
The sooner she found the file or ensured that it was
not in the house, the sooner she could be on her
way.

Moving soundlessly, she eased across the hall to
her uncle's room. After closing the door, she felt her
way along the bed until she'd reached the night table. Inside the top drawer was a flashlight. For a few
seconds she could only sit there and inhale the scent
of her uncle. His unmade bed still held the sweet
spicy smell of his aftershave. She squeezed her eyes
shut to block the renewed sting of tears. Shaking her
head to clear it, she opened her eyes and forced herself to focus on the task at hand. There was no time
for any more grieving. The best thing she could do
for her uncle now was bring his killer to justice. To
do that, she needed that file.

Using the narrow beam of the flashlight, she
searched her uncle's bedroom from top to bottom.
Every drawer, the closet, the bed, the backs of mir-
rors, behind pictures on the wall and inside the
frames. *Nada.* If the file was in the house, it was not
in his bedroom.

Shutting off the light, she made her way back to
the guest room and went through the same routine.
Again she found nothing except a few fuzz bunnies

in the back of the closet. Grabbing her duffel, she headed for the bathroom. If Max had heard her moving around, which he most likely had, he'd just think she was up early and preparing for the day.

If the gods were on her side, he wouldn't know she planned to leave until she was already gone.

MAX LISTENED to Scout move about, instinctively poised to go after her if she made a run for it, until he heard the spray of water in the shower. Then he relaxed. Since she hadn't checked to see if he was up, he had to assume she wanted to be left alone. That was fine by him. He didn't want to intrude on her solitude. Well, that wasn't exactly true. The bottom line was that he didn't feel quite prepared to face her just yet.

Pushing himself to his feet, he straightened his shirt and tugged on his shoulder holster. She could probably use a strong cup of coffee, the same as he could. That, at least, would give him an opening line when she emerged from the shower.

Max plowed his fingers through his hair and maneuvered his way through the kitchen. Flipping on the light, he thought about how he'd hardly slept at all for fear she'd take off on him. He glanced at the digital clock on the microwave and noted that it was only 5:00 a.m. He doubted Scout had had much sleep, either. But she was up now, and so was he.

If he was honest with himself he'd admit here and now that it wouldn't have mattered if she'd been chained and shackled last night. He still wouldn't have slept, not with his mind torturing him with perpetual replays of every moment they'd spent together four months ago. Tension had simmered just beneath the surface all night long as his senses recalled the feel of her...the taste of her.

Max shivered and forced his mind to focus on the coffeemaker. He had a job to do. Scout needed him to do that job. End of subject.

He filled the carafe with water and set it aside while he located the filters and the coffee. Once a filter was in the basket, he opened the large red tin of coffee and snagged the scoop by the handle. He dug deeply into the rich, dark grounds, then frowned. The scoop caught on something. He stirred the grounds, digging more deeply, his heartbeat kicking into high gear.

Paper enclosed in a plastic resealable bag poked up from the bottom of the can. Max reached in, gripping the corner with his thumb and forefinger. He edged the can toward the sink and dragged the plastic bag out, allowing the coffee to scatter in the sink rather than on the counter. He shook off the remaining grounds and inspected the contents of the bag through the plastic. The documents were folded in half, with the blank side showing.

His brow furrowed in concentration, Max carefully opened the bag and pulled the pages out by one corner. No one hid documents in his coffee can unless he didn't want them found. And there was no reason to hide something unless it contained incriminating evidence.

This had to be the file Scout was looking for.

Max paused to listen for the sound of spraying water. She was still in the shower. Good. He wanted a chance to look at her uncle's evidence before he had to hand it over to her. If Harold Atkins, her uncle, the man who thought of her as a daughter, really did have evidence that Alexon had held her against her will or was involved in some wrongdoing where Scout was concerned, Max would bring in every last one of those involved.

But first he had to be sure it really was Alexon. The company had warned him that a competitor was in a race to develop the antidote first. Maybe Alexon was only trying to protect Scout. There was simply no way for him to be sure yet.

The plastic bag contained three pages. He opened each folded page and flattened it on the counter. Scrubbing his hand over his stubbled jaw, he studied each in turn. The craving for morning coffee slowly seeped out of conscious thought. His entire physical being stilled as he read the words again and then again in an effort to absorb fully all that they meant.

"...After years of research the answer to our K-141 dilemma has appeared to us completely by accident. With the mother's immunity on record, it is without doubt that the key to the antidote lies in the stem cells of the unborn child. These cells must be harvested by whatever means possible...."

Max blinked. This couldn't mean... *It's me they want...just me....*

He reread the pages. "...With the mother's immunity on record...stem cells of the unborn child..."

His gut clenched.

Scout was pregnant.

Adrenaline sent his heart into a faster rhythm as he searched for a date on the documents. There was none, no indication of when this decision had been made. She'd said that Alexon had been holding her prisoner. But she didn't look pregnant, so surely she couldn't be very far along. And certainly it had taken a few weeks for her to discover that she was pregnant. Max exhaled a disgusted breath and rubbed his forehead. Maybe not. With today's technology, wasn't it possible to discover a pregnancy within days of conception?

He swore. How the hell did he know? He hadn't thought about pregnancies or kids. He'd expected marriage to come first. The realization that he hadn't used protection with Scout while they were in isolation slammed into his brain. And why would he? They were supposed to be dying! He blinked rapidly and fought the shock grabbing him by the throat.

Okay. Hold up. Maybe he was jumping the gun here. There was the old boyfriend. Gage what's-his-name. Max gritted his teeth to hold back a string of expletives at just the thought of the guy.

He couldn't think about that right now. He had to know if Scout really was pregnant and…

What was he thinking? Yes! She was pregnant. The proof was right here on paper. Sure, it didn't state her name, but he knew. She was the "mother" who'd proved to be immune to K-141. No one they knew of had survived it until he and Scout had.

So the only real question here was whose child was she carrying? The document didn't mention paternity. If Max was the father, wouldn't his own immunity be mentioned?

Feeling suddenly numb, he folded the pages and stuffed them into his back pocket. He had to know what this meant. Anticipation abruptly hurtled through his veins, ushering him forward until he reached the hall and beat against the still-closed bathroom door. Was *this* what she'd been holding back?

"Scout! We need to talk!"

If she was carrying his child and she hadn't told him... Fury whipped through him. Why would she let all this time pass and so many events transpire and not give him a chance to help? She had to know that he cared. That he would be there for her...for their child.

The truth hit him then. Because he'd walked away just as she had. Sure, he'd tried to call a couple of times, but he hadn't put forth any real effort. He hadn't wanted to go out on that limb alone. If she'd wanted to continue a relationship she would have said something, called...or returned his call.

He pounded on the door once more. "Scout, come on out of there. We need to talk!"

No answer. He frowned. The water continued to shower down beyond the door, but there was no other sound.

Yet another epiphany hit him and he tried the door. It wasn't locked. He shoved it open, allowing it to bang against the wall as he barged into the steamy room. He jerked the shower curtain to one side, and his latest assumption proved accurate.

She was gone.

Max shut off the water and stormed back into the hall. He checked both bedrooms and found the window in her uncle's room open. He'd already noted her duffel was missing from the room where she'd slept. But her "home office" bag was still there. Obviously it didn't contain anything important—or if it had, she'd have taken that with her.

Grinding his teeth to hold back a litany of self-deprecating curses, he started to climb through the window, but a sound echoing down the hall stopped him.

He paused, listened intently.

The sound reached him again.

Front door…knob turning.

Someone was trying to get in the house. It was still pretty dark outside even with the tendrils of dawn reaching from the east. Drawing his weapon, Max eased into the hall. One thing was certain, it sure as hell wouldn't be Scout. Whoever it was, Max didn't have time to play games. He had to get on Scout's trail. She couldn't have gotten far.

Just as he reached the front door, it swung inward.

Instinctively he leveled his weapon on the intruder.

The shiny steel barrel of a Beretta nine-millimeter stared back at him. Beyond the hand gripping the butt of the weapon stood a man—not quite as tall as Max and with dark features. He seemed as startled to see Max as Max no doubt looked at seeing him.

"Who the hell are you?" the intruder rasped.

Max didn't flinch as he stared more fully into those dark eyes. "Since you're the one doing the breaking and entering I think maybe you'd better identify yourself first."

"This is Harold Atkins's house. Unless you're a long-lost son I'm unaware of, I can't imagine what business you have here," the stranger retorted just as boldly.

Max didn't have time for this crap. He cocked his weapon. "Who are you?"

The stranger's conviction faded visibly. "I'm Gage Kimble. I'm looking for Scout."

Gage.

The ex-boyfriend. The one Scout had been on the rebound from four months ago. Former special forces. He worked in personal security now, if Max recalled correctly. Max disliked the other man on sight. He was most likely the reason she'd walked away from Max so easily. And probably why she hadn't bothered to return his calls.

Why was he showing up now? Scout hadn't mentioned him.

"Why do you want to see her?" Max demanded. He wanted to kick himself when the curtness of his own tone reflected exactly how jealous he felt at the moment. He'd expected Gage to be some jerk who was most comfortable on a sofa watching a ball game. What he hadn't expected was a guy who looked every bit as fit as Max himself, and who sported a weapon just as lethal as the one Max now held pointed at Gage's face.

Something changed in the guy's eyes. Still hovering in the open doorway, he glanced to his right, then leveled a piercing gaze on Max. "She isn't here, is she?"

"Why would you say that?" He didn't have time for this. He had to get rid of this guy.

"Were you driving a gray sedan with Illinois plates?"

Another surge of adrenaline burned through Max.

Before he could answer, Gage said, "That car just pulled out about two houses down."

Max swore.

"If you'd like to give chase," Gage offered,

abruptly lowering his weapon, ''my Range Rover is waiting at the curb.''

''What makes you think I'd go anywhere with you?'' Max growled. He hadn't liked this guy before he'd met him. He sure as hell didn't now.

Gage shrugged. ''I don't know. Maybe because she's getting away from both of us.''

''Let's go.'' Max lowered his weapon, but didn't reholster it. He wasn't about to let his guard down where this guy was concerned.

Before Max had even closed the passenger side door, the SUV squealed into motion. Gage Kimble drove swiftly through the quiet streets, easily catching sight of the sedan once more. But she was still well ahead of them. They rounded the next corner and she was gone. Both swearing, and with Kimble pushing the SUV for all it was worth, they discovered, several hard maneuvers later, the sedan parked in front of a warehouse, the driver's door still open.

They searched the area thoroughly, but Scout was nowhere to be found. She'd vanished. Max had an uneasy feeling about her sudden disappearance. Part of him was convinced that she was still in the vicinity, but another part of him was certain she was gone.

Dammit. Why hadn't she trusted him?

He glared as Kimble returned to his Range Rover. And why the hell had this guy shown up?

''I didn't find anything,'' he said, shaking his head in disgust. ''She's given us the slip.''

Max rounded on him then. ''Why don't you tell me what your interest in Scout is?'' He still held his weapon in his right hand. Unlike Kimble, he had no intention of behaving so nonchalantly in the presence of a stranger. Especially not when that stranger was Scout's ex-boyfriend. Her lover... Max clenched his jaw until a muscle flexed there.

A full ten tension-filled seconds ticked by as Kimble stared back at him, clearly weighing his words and attempting to determine just who Max was. "You never said who you are," he finally countered, with utter confidence that he had every right to know the answer.

"Pierce Maxwell. I'm with the Colby Agency." Max managed to relay the information without shooting the guy for emphasis. He had never had this much difficulty regaining his perspective on a matter.

Kimble smiled knowingly. "Ah yes. Max. The gentleman she spent those three weeks in isolation with." He nodded, another knowing gesture. "She told me about you."

Max narrowed his gaze. "When did she tell you about me?" Dammit, he'd known it. She'd gone right back to this jerk. Even after what they'd shared.

The other man crossed his arms over his chest and leaned casually against his overpriced SUV. "Oh, a couple weeks after she was released. We had dinner at one of our old favorite haunts in Houston."

Okay. Dinner. They'd had dinner. He was an old friend of her father's, Max remembered. Maybe he was making more out of this than it was. He had to get a grip here. He had to ditch this guy and find Scout.

"Well, thanks for sharing," he said with a smile, his tone leaving no doubt as to what he was really thinking. "But I need to be off. Places to go and people to see and all that.'' The keys were in the sedan. He'd take it back to the office and pick up his SUV, then he had to put a call in to Cooper. Scout would most likely head back to Houston. Or, at the very least, she'd probably try and contact her assistant.

''We don't have to be enemies, you know,'' Kimble offered. He straightened from the vehicle.

Max tensed, his fingers tightening around the butt of his weapon.

Kimble smiled as if he'd noted Max's reaction and was amused by it. Max was not amused. In fact, he was about as far from amused as was humanly possible to get.

''Really, Max, old man,'' Kimble said jovially, ''you should learn to relax.'' His gaze turned suddenly hard and serious, but when he spoke, his voice remained low and amicable. ''I need to find her. I won't allow anything to stand in my way.''

Max knew a threat when he heard one. It was his turn to smile then. ''What'd she do? Break a date with you or something?'' Again Max had to clench his jaw hard to prevent himself from saying more. His rigid posture and tight tone were already giving away far too much.

''She's pregnant.'' Kimble's expression changed, relaxed into an unreadable mask. ''The child is mine.''

Shock radiated all the way down to the soles of Max's feet. A hurt or disappointment he couldn't quite label shuddered through him. The child wasn't his. She had gone back to her ex when she'd walked away from him, without looking back.

''I don't know why she's on the run,'' Kimble

added, his face still wiped clean of all emotion. "But I want to help her. To help our child."

Something dark and unfathomable welled up inside Max. For the first time in his life he wanted to kill a man. A man he scarcely knew and with whom he had no beef. Except one.

Somehow, without flinching, Max said, "I'll give her your message when I see her."

Kimble climbed into his SUV. The final look he gave Max before driving away said more than any words could have.

This wasn't over.

Chapter Eight

Scout held her breath as she felt the car dip slightly with the driver's weight. The engine started and then the vehicle rolled into forward motion. She exhaled softly, thankful that her plan had worked.

Though it was dark in the trunk, she could deal with it. Her right foot was bare. The sneaker lay on the floor next to her, and her sock now served as a block preventing the trunk's latch from engaging. All she had to do was keep the lid from bouncing until he stopped again, which wasn't so bad, since they were on city streets and not bumpy country roads.

She strained to listen when she heard Max's voice as he spoke to someone. Via his cellular phone, she supposed. She hadn't been able to make out the conversation he'd had outside a few moments ago. Someone had helped him give chase…but who? No one was supposed to know where they were. Had he lied about Cooper's whereabouts?

"Yeah, Cooper, this is Max." Pause. "I've lost her. Keep a close eye on that assistant, since Scout may call." There was a pause. A long, frustrated sigh. "That'll work."

Scout tried not to be affected by the sound of his voice, but she always was. There was just something about that husky baritone that made her weak in the knees—even at a time like this. She was so truly pathetic. She'd been in love with Max since the moment she'd laid eyes on him. That she now carried his child only made her love him more.

But she couldn't trust him completely. Not yet. Alexon had hired him. Max had a strong sense of loyalty. To be disloyal to Alexon would, in effect, make him disloyal to the Colby Agency. She knew the agency's reputation, they couldn't know what Alexon was up to. She didn't see that happening. And if Cooper wasn't the one to provide his backup transportation, which evidently he was not, then who had? She listened intently as Max spoke again.

"Oh, yeah. I found that file she was looking for. The one her uncle had hidden...."

The rest of the conversation faded into insignificance. Ice slid through her veins. He knew she was pregnant now. Worse, he'd lied to her. He'd searched the kitchen and the living room and supposedly come up empty-handed. She remembered the encouraging words he'd said to her when he'd tucked her into bed. *I'm sure we'll find that file.* He'd already found it. He knew her secret.

Well, now she knew something, too.

She couldn't trust Max at all.

He was one of the enemy.

Her anxiety ratcheted up a notch. Everything was falling apart. She hadn't expected Max's help. Hadn't wanted it. But she hadn't anticipated him being in the enemy's camp, either. There was no doubt in her mind now that he was exactly that.

Somehow Alexon managed to keep tabs on their whereabouts—just another nail in the coffin of her trust. No way would Alexon have known where she and Max ended up last night if he hadn't kept them informed. No way. And it had to be one of Alexon's men who'd brought him hunting for her when she'd left with the sedan. There had been no other transportation, and Cooper was obviously in Houston. Her uncle's car was still in Alexon's parking lot, where he'd left it the morning before his death.

A spear of pain arced through her at the thought of her uncle. This was too much. Scout squeezed her eyes shut and blocked the suddenly overwhelming need to simply give up.

No!

Her eyes snapped open.

She wasn't done yet. She would not let anyone, not Alexon, not even Max, stop her.

Twenty minutes later, Max braked the sedan again. This time he got out of the car and opened the rear driver's side door. Something dragged across the back seat. Then he slammed the door.

Her duffel, she realized. He was taking it with him.

That was okay by her. She had clothes on her back. There was nothing in the duffel of particular importance. What she'd left behind in her tote bag, even the file on Alexon, held nothing of significant value. None of it proved anything. It all boiled down to her word against theirs.

But Harold's file was another matter.

She wanted that file.

She would have it.

When she heard another door open she made her

move. She allowed the trunk lid to fly open and she bounded out, landing on her feet and taking off at a dead run. She was at Max's back and had the barrel of her weapon pressed against his head before he could turn around. The fact that he'd been loading her duffel into his SUV had been to her advantage.

"Give me the file," she demanded without preamble. Why beat around the bush? She knew what she was dealing with now. There was no point in pretending.

Dawn was streaking across the nearly deserted parking lot. They were back at the building that housed the Colby Agency. The sedan she'd exited as well as another in the same color sat next to an SUV. Max had parked the sedan directly behind his own SUV, which had facilitated her ability to come up behind him with such ease.

"Scout, listen to me. You've got to trust me," he said in that voice that had haunted her dreams for four long months.

She laughed. Couldn't help herself. "Trust you? Trust you?!" Hysteria rose in her voice with each word she uttered. "Just how stupid do you think I am, Maxwell?"

"Listen to me—" He made a move to turn around, but she stopped him with a jab of the barrel.

"Don't move," she said from between clenched teeth. "And put your hands up where I can see them." How could she have allowed herself to fall in love with this guy? She blinked back the tears brimming. He'd fooled her completely. She'd cared about Gage, but she'd seen through him to a degree all along. He'd never owned her heart the way Max had.

What a fool she'd been.

"Just take it easy," he urged softly, using that lady-killer voice to rattle her. "I'm not the enemy, Scout."

She scoffed. "You are something, Pierce Maxwell, I'll give you that. But I've got your number now, so give me the file."

"Your friend told me about the pregnancy."

His voice was still soft, but there was an underlying tension that was both unmistakable and unnerving.

He knew she was pregnant with his child, and all he could do was say "Your friend told me...."

A frown creased her brow, adding another layer of tension to the headache already pounding in her skull. "What friend? What the hell are you talking about, Maxwell?" The file had told him her secret.

"Gage Kimble," he said flatly. "He told me."

Gage? When had Max seen Gage? "What does Gage have to do with this?" She nudged him with the barrel once more. "I'm sure you discovered I was pregnant when you found the file. Why lie about it? Now, give it to me!"

"He also told me," Max added, so maddeningly calm that she wanted to scream, "that the child was his."

To say the announcement shocked her would have been a vast understatement. Gage had told Max that she was carrying *his* child? That was insane. Why would he say such a thing? How could Gage even know about the baby? Maybe Max was simply baiting her to get the truth. She opened her mouth to set the record straight about Gage, but snapped it shut instead. This was perfect. Though she still couldn't fathom where Max had run into Gage or why, at least now her secret was safe for a little while longer. She would simply allow Max to believe what he would. A twinge of regret flickered through her, but she ignored it. He didn't deserve to know. Sure, he was the baby's father, but she couldn't trust him. He was the enemy now.

"I don't care what he told you. Just give me the file."

"It's in my back pocket."

Scout swallowed with difficulty. She didn't relish the idea of touching him. Well, the real problem was she knew what her physical reaction would be, and she didn't want that. But she did want the file. She had to have it.

Firming her resolve, she reached beneath his sport jacket and checked first one jeans pocket and then the other. The one on the right bulged slightly with his wallet. The left yielded only a few folded pages. She quickly unfolded them and glanced downward.

"This is all?" she demanded, certain there must be more. The way her uncle had talked, he had irrefutable evidence on why she was being sought and by whom. Of course, that would be Alexon. They were the ones who'd held her hostage. That's where her uncle had worked. It was all quite simple...and more costly than anything should be.

"I found those pages buried in the canister this morning when I got up to make coffee," he explained. "You were in the shower...or I thought you were," he added, disappointment echoing in his voice.

"Like I'd believe anything you said," she muttered. What should she do with him now? She arched a speculative brow. She could lock him in the trunk of the sedan.

"I haven't lied to you, Scout," he insisted, looking over his shoulder at her, those blues eyes beseeching her for the one thing she wouldn't give him—her trust.

Firming her grip on the nine-millimeter, she issued one last demand before leaving him for good. "If you haven't lied to me, then why is it that Alexon shows up every time I'm with you? There's no way they could have known we'd go to my uncle's house. You had to have tipped them off."

He shook his head, the movement drawing her attention to all that thick blond hair. It was the color of wet sand and begged to have her fingers run through it. But that would never happen again.

"I haven't contacted Alexon since I found you. That's the truth, whether you choose to believe it or not."

"Yeah, right," she snapped. "Like they just happened to show up this morning at 5:30 a.m. when I was making my escape."

Max turned slightly to look at her. She nudged him with the weapon. He flinched, but didn't back off. "That wasn't Alexon. That was your boyfriend, *Gage.*"

He said the name with blatant disdain. But it wasn't his pointed annoyance that grabbed her attention, it was the bald-faced lie.

"Why would Gage show up at my uncle's house?" she retorted, disgusted with herself for even pursuing the subject. "I haven't—"

Before she could finish the statement that she hadn't seen Gage in months, Max interrupted with

a flare of temper. "It was him. He showed up looking for you. When you took off we followed in his
vehicle."

She tried to think what kind of car Gage had
driven the last time she saw him, but nothing came.
Their relationship had been over for months. When
he'd asked her to dinner shortly after her release
from isolation, she'd gone out with him only to get
her mind off Max. Then she hadn't seen Gage again.

"I didn't know the two of you were pals," she
spat, suddenly suspicious of the coincidence. Sure,
Gage knew where her uncle lived. But why show
up now? After all this time?

"Trust me," Max said, his tone, his expression
nothing short of deadly, "we're not."

This was all entirely too confusing and she had
no time for any of it. She shoved the pages into her
jeans pocket and motioned toward the sedan with
her weapon. "Give me your gun and then climb into
the trunk."

He turned all the way around to face her, making
her take an unexpected step back. Only then did she
remember that she was minus one shoe.

"I'm not giving you my weapon and I'm damn
sure not climbing into the trunk of that car."

Why was it men always thought that women
weren't serious when they gave an order?

"You might want to rethink that, Maxwell." She
smiled saccharinely. "After all, I'm the one holding
the gun."

He glanced at her weapon, then back at her, a hint
of a smile lingering around the corners of his sexy
mouth. "You're not going to shoot me."

Fury streaked through her and she cocked the

weapon before she could think better of it. "Says who?" She lifted an eyebrow.

Now she had him. He looked decidedly more accommodating.

"Put the weapon down, Scout," he suggested. "I know you don't want to do this. Let's talk about it."

"I'm through talking to you." She jerked her head in the direction of the sedan. "Now, let's go."

"Drop the weapon."

The male voice came from right behind her, and she felt the nudge of a cold steel barrel on the back of her neck. Now she had a dilemma.

"I don't think so," she replied. Heck, what did she have to lose? Maybe Alexon didn't give a rat's tail about Max's life, but they did want her in one piece. They wouldn't kill her.

Three things happened in the next few seconds. Something passed between the two men; Scout saw it in Max's eyes. A bout of morning sickness hit her—so hard that she had to slap her left hand over her mouth. And her right arm was suddenly knocked upward, forcing her aim away from Max.

When a second wave of nausea hit she would have dropped her weapon entirely if the man behind her hadn't snagged it from her hand. She made a mad dash for the rear of the SUV and broke into a fit of dry heaves.

She could hear Max and the other man talking, but she couldn't stop heaving long enough to do anything about it. Since she hadn't consumed anything since last night there wasn't much to lose, but the spasms plagued her for several more minutes. She wished for water and for crackers, about the only things she could safely eat and drink in the mornings. God, this part was supposed to be over by now.

"You okay?" Max moved up behind her, his tone filled with concern.

"Of course I'm not okay," she griped. She wiped her trembling lips with the back of her hand and tried to ignore the sour taste in her mouth. But that was nothing compared to the reality that it was over; she was caught. Max wasn't here to help her. She would never be able to bring her uncle's killer to justice.

And she'd failed.

Failed to keep her baby safe.

"We should go inside."

The other man was speaking. Scout glanced in his direction, but didn't recognize him. He was tall, dark and entirely too handsome to be a bad guy. But he had to be. He and Max were in this together. They both, no doubt, worked for Alexon.

Max nodded toward the other man. "This is Simon Ruhl. He's also with the Colby Agency."

If that was supposed to make her feel any better, it didn't.

"Did Alexon hire you, as well?" she asked of the enigmatic man watching her so studiously. That dark gaze cut briefly to Max.

"Miss Jackson," Ruhl said, the voice every bit as dark and mysterious as he appeared, "it would be best if we continued this discussion inside."

It wasn't as if she had a choice, but when Max reached for her arm, she jerked away from him. He shrugged and waited for her to walk ahead of him.

"I need my shoe."

Max looked startled to see that she wore only one

runner. His gaze went from eyes to her feet and back. "What happened to it?"

"Trade secret." She turned her back and marched over to the sedan. The trunk lid was still up so she simply reached inside and retrieved her sock and sneaker. Bracing her weight against the car, she tugged on first one and then the other. The two men waited impatiently a few feet away. They looked anywhere but at her as if what she was doing was intensely personal. Men…she'd never understand what made them tick.

The three entered the building and boarded the elevator. Scout's stomach roiled again with the upward movement. Her head was pounding and she was sure any minute now she'd be sick again. What else could go wrong? *Don't ask,* she scolded herself. She really, really didn't want to know.

"Do you need a physician, Miss Jackson?" Simon Ruhl asked.

"She's fine," Max said pointedly before she could answer.

The two men exchanged looks again. Max seemed as mad as hell; Simon simply appeared bemused. Why couldn't the fathers have the morning sickness? Scout thought, tossing a glare in Max's direction.

When the elevator doors opened, Scout was the first to move. She needed a drink and a ladies' room. Now. But she stopped abruptly, realizing she had no clue where the ladies' room was.

"I need—"

She didn't have to say the rest. Max pointed to the end of a long corridor. "On the left."

He followed a few yards behind her. Though his

steps were muffled by the luxurious carpet, and she didn't look back, she could feel him watching her. Let him think what he would. It was for the best that he didn't know the truth. If she couldn't trust him with her life, why would she trust him with her child's?

She slipped into the powder room and closed the door behind her before taking a moment to lean against it. She shut her eyes and tried to stop the spinning that had suddenly started in her head. She needed food, but she wasn't sure she could hold it down. She needed sleep, but that was impossible at the moment.

A tremble ran through her and she fought the urge to give in to tears. She'd done more than her share of that lately. Hormones, she reasoned. She was pregnant, after all. Seeing Max again didn't help. She'd thought she was over him...but now she knew better. She would never be over him. No matter how he betrayed her.

Bolstering her resolve with a deep breath, she pushed away from the door and took care of necessary business. She washed her face and rinsed her mouth until the bitter taste was gone, then took a long drink of water, praying it would stay down. She waited for a while just to make sure before leaving the confines of the elegant ladies' room. It would likely be her only reprieve from what was to come. The man outside the door would want answers.

Max waited in the hall. He started to knock again, but forced himself to be patient. It wasn't easy. He was edgy and damn worried about her.

He didn't understand the intensity of the worry. It wasn't even his child she was carrying. He shouldn't feel anything beyond basic human compassion. Certainly not the raging jealously currently ripping his insides to shreds. When he thought about the jerk who'd shown up at her uncle's house this morning, he wanted to hit something.

Was she still in love with Gage?

Max closed his eyes and blew out a breath. Who she loved or didn't love was not his business. Learning about the pregnancy should have given him a clearer perspective on the woman. Instead it had only unbalanced him further. How could he still feel this way, knowing she was expecting another man's child?

Maybe Kimble had taken advantage of her. "And maybe you're an idiot," Max muttered.

"Everything all right?" Simon stopped a few feet away, conscious of Max's need for space at the moment, but, at the same time, concerned for his co-worker, who was very obviously losing control.

Max shrugged. "We have issues to clear up before Alexon is alerted to her whereabouts."

Simon nodded. "Cooper is still in Houston?"

"Yeah. He was supposed to come back today, but I asked him to stay awhile longer." *Since I thought we'd lost Scout,* Max didn't add.

Simon read people too well. He knew something was very wrong, but he was too much of a gentleman to make the accusation. Simon Ruhl was former FBI and had worked his way up the food chain very quickly at the Colby Agency. He served as second in command whenever Ian Michaels was away. Though he worked cases regularly himself, he was briefed daily by Ian and Victoria as to the status of all ongoing investigations.

"It's a good thing I decided to come to the office early this morning," he said, giving Max the opportunity to explain what had happened in the parking lot without having to ask.

"We had a little disagreement," Max hedged. There was no point in going into all the details. Simon had no way of knowing what a wildcat Scout could be. Max would get the situation back under control. Eventually.

Simon nodded again. "Let me know if there's anything you need."

"Sure thing." Max watched as he walked away. There were guys who were slick and there were guys who were smooth. Simon Ruhl was both. He knew Max wasn't giving him the whole story, but he trusted him to do the right thing.

Now, if Max could just gain Scout's trust. He wasn't completely sure what he'd done to lose it in the first place, but whatever it was, he had to find a way to win her over. It was the only way they were ever going to get anywhere with this investigation. He and Scout needed to go someplace safe and private to have a long heart-to-heart talk. Too much between them needed settling. Alexon wouldn't wait forever. They would want results soon.

Max didn't want to be faced with a decision between betraying Scout and betraying the agency.

That was the last thing he wanted.

With his patience running thin, he turned back to the door and raised his fist to knock. The door opened before he could.

"I'm ready to go now," Scout announced solemnly.

A frown aggravated the headache throbbing beneath his brow. "Go where?" What the hell was she up to now?

She looked up at him, those big gray eyes filled with resignation. "You're going to turn me over to Alexon, aren't you?" She shrugged wearily. "I can't win. Do what you have to do. I won't hold it against you. You're only doing your job." When he would have spoken, she added, "I'd do the same thing if Alexon had hired me to find you."

She had to rub it in. She couldn't see that he'd already pushed Alexon to the limit by refusing to bring her in immediately. "Just come with me," he growled. He wanted to grab her by the arm, drag her to his office and give her a firm shake, but he knew if he touched her he'd lose even more of his objectivity. Instead, he pivoted and led the way, watching from the corner of his eye to make sure she followed. He wasn't about to trust her again not to run. They had reached the proverbial Mexican standoff. Neither of them wanted to trust the other.

Once he'd closed the door, blocking out all else, he gestured to a chair and she settled into it, her head held high, her shoulders squared despite her melodramatic display of surrender.

Even her posture made him furious.

Rather than pace as he desperately needed to, Max forced himself to sit down on the edge of his desk, well above her eye level, and then focus his full attention on her. He was in charge now. She needed to know that. He wasn't swallowing the "I surrender" act for a second.

"Start from the beginning," he directed curtly, "and tell me every little thing, no matter how seemingly insignificant, that happened from the moment we parted ways four months ago until we met again in the cemetery.''

She turned suddenly a little green around the gills. He recognized the look. He'd seen it before when she'd made that abrupt dash for the rear of his SUV.

''If I don't eat something I'm pretty sure I might throw up again,'' she said bluntly.

Max opened his mouth to reply, but before he could find the right words, she launched herself from her chair and lunged for the wastebasket between his desk and credenza. She heaved violently. His own stomach tensed in sympathy.

After a moment she straightened and offered him a wobbly smile. ''Too late.''

Chapter Nine

Max waited patiently while Scout nibbled on the snack crackers and sipped a cola. Once he'd settled her in the lounge next to the reception area, he'd put in a call to Cooper to let him know he could return to Chicago. Max would likely need him for backup surveillance.

He tried his level best not to dwell on the idea that Scout was pregnant, or on the jerk, Kimble, who'd fathered the child. The strangest sensation swelled inside Max every time he thought about the two of them together. He knew it was jealousy plain and simple, but the ferocity of it startled him. He'd known all along that something special had sparked between him and Scout four months ago. Apparently he hadn't realized just how deeply the emotion had gone, on his part, anyway. She hadn't felt the same, obviously. If she had, surely she wouldn't have run immediately into another man's arms.

Max closed his eyes and pushed away that line of thinking. He had to stay focused on the case. No matter whose child she carried, she needed his help—though she clearly didn't realize it yet. If her safety was truly Alexon's primary agenda, Max had to convince her of that. If, as she believed, Alexon was the enemy, he had to keep her safe. And the baby as well, he added ruefully, until he could prove it.

"I got the first call about three or four weeks after we were released," she said, breaking the long minutes of silence between them.

She stood, picked up her soft-drink can and food wrapper and deposited them in the nearby trash receptacle. Taking her time, as if considering carefully what she wanted to say next, she resumed her seat.

"For more than a month they sent someone to me regularly or had me drop by a local Houston lab to provide blood samples and the like. They even flew me up here a couple of times." A frown marred the smoothness of her pale brow.

Unbidden, the urge to reach out and caress away the troubling lines bloomed inside Max. He resisted.

"You agreed without question?" he asked suddenly. That would be so unlike the woman he'd thought he'd known in that jungle, and then in isolation four months ago.

She drew a heavy breath and released it slowly. "No. I questioned the necessity right away, but they kept insisting that it was essential to my continued good health." She looked directly at him then. "They told me you were doing the same thing."

He shook his head, his own brow furrowing in confusion. "Until a few days ago I hadn't heard from Alexon since they released us."

"Well, that's what they told me, anyway. Then, about two months ago, they insisted I fly to Chicago again for further evaluation. They said you'd be there, as well. I figured I could drop by and see my uncle while I was in town, so I agreed without much convincing.'' She shrugged. ''It seemed like the right thing to do at the time.

''They held me against my will for six weeks.'' She shook her head. ''Uncle Harold finally realized what they had done and rescued me. He was helping me escape and they killed him.''

Max's gut clenched every time he heard the harrowing story. If he found out that Alexon had lied to him… Though he couldn't imagine they could be that dirty without Victoria's knowledge. ''But you managed to avoid being recaptured,'' he prodded, needing to hear the rest.

She nodded. ''They hadn't expected me to fight like a man.'' She smiled. ''I took two of them down before I ditched the others.'' Her smile faded instantly. ''I didn't get the one who killed my uncle. I can't ID his face, since they were all dressed in black, including ski masks, but I know his voice and the way he moves.'' Her gaze connected with Max's once more, and the savagery burning there unsettled him. ''But I will find him before this is over.''

Max didn't doubt her for a moment. He knew the kind of resolve she possessed. The men who'd come after them at his cabin had been dressed exactly the way she described. ''And your boyfriend,'' he began cautiously. ''Where was he while this was all going on?'' She'd told him they'd only had dinner that once. Had dinner turned into something else and resulted in the child she now carried? Fury boiled up in Max. He tamped it down. He had to stay cool on the subject or risk losing the unsteady ground he'd gained in the last few minutes.

She looked away now, unable or unwilling to

maintain eye contact. "We only saw each other that once, shortly after I was released." She looked at Max then, looked him straight in the eye and said without hesitation, "But that's all it was…just that once."

Whatever point she was trying to make was lost on Max in his present condition of teetering between outrage and all-consuming jealousy. "I understand that once is all it takes."

Her cheeks flushed, and he didn't miss the flare of anger in her eyes. She jerked from her pocket the folded pages he'd found at her uncle's house, and spread them on the table. Taking her time, she carefully smoothed out the creases and studied the information written there.

"This proves that Alexon intended to snatch my baby at all costs," she said, pushing the documents toward him. "How can you still believe they aren't involved?"

Max reviewed all three pages with painstaking thoroughness. The papers documented the numerous tests confirming her pregnancy and the results of various blood tests. And then there was the note stating that the child was to be secured at all costs. But the documents did not carry Alexon's logo on the letterhead. In fact, there was no heading on any of the pages. There were no identifying marks whatsoever. It just didn't make sense that Alexon would hire a firm as reputable as the Colby Agency if they were carrying on these kinds of underhanded tactics behind the scenes. Their treachery was bound to be discovered by a competent firm. Why would they murder her uncle and then give him a high-class send-off?

At last Max looked up from the documents, and Scout found herself holding her breath, waiting for his decision. Would he believe her? And help her bring down Alexon?

"I want to believe you, Scout." He probed her with that blue gaze and she recognized the sincerity there. "But there's nothing here that ties the documents to Alexon. I'm not saying Alexon isn't involved on some level, but we can't prove they're the bad guys. It's still your word against theirs."

She shoved back her chair, the legs scraping across the slick marble, and stood. Glaring down at him, she forced as much fury into her voice as she could muster. "And, of course, we both know who you believe. Why don't you just go ahead and turn me over to them now? Why pretend you're going to help me? Just do what they're paying you to, and stop playing games with me!" The rising hysteria in her voice took most of the conviction out of her fury, but it was the best she could do. By the time the final words were spoken she was shaking like a frightened child. She hated this sense of helplessness.

Why had he barged back into her life? She could have gone on pretending she didn't care if the father of her child was ever involved in their lives. She could have continued to fool herself into thinking that she didn't care about him. It had been nothing but a volatile combination of stress and lust that brought them together in the first place. But no, he'd had to come charging in like a superhero, and now she could no longer deny the truth she'd hidden from herself.

She needed Max on a very personal level.

Worse than that, she wanted him.

And he was the enemy.

Slowly, he stood and moved around to her side of the table. For one long moment he simply stood next to her, allowing her to feel the heat and strength he emanated. Finally, he reached out and took one of her hands in his. She started to resist, but she was just too tired to fight anymore. Still, she refused to look at him. She could feel his gaze on her face, but she wouldn't return it. Couldn't look back.

He wrapped those long, strong fingers around hers and spoke softly to her. "Scout, I'm not playing games with you. I want to help you." He squeezed her hand, sending tendrils of heat searing through her that tugged at her already jumbled emotions. "I promise I'll keep you safe until we figure this out. I swear I won't let anyone hurt you."

She peered up at him then. "And my baby," she demanded, her voice trembling, "will you protect my baby, as well?"

"With my life."

She knew he meant what he said. Max would not give his word lightly. She had learned that about him four months ago. He'd sworn to protect her and her child. She had to trust that. They were still on shaky ground on some levels, and things were far too complicated for her to tell him the truth about the baby just yet, but they were making progress. For that, she was immensely relieved. For the first time in her adult life, she admitted to herself that she truly needed someone.

And right now, that someone was Max.

"So what do we do? How can we prove Alexon did this?"

Max considered her question for a moment, but didn't relax his grip. She kind of liked the feel of his big strong hand engulfing hers.

"The agency has numerous pieces of correspondence from Alexon relevant to cases we've worked for them in the past. We can have our analysts determine if the paper, print and ink match up. Also, we can compare the handwritten notes in the margins to any signatures we have on file."

"Does this mean that you believe me now?" She told herself not to hope, but foolishly, she did.

"It means," he clarified patiently, "that I believe someone is determined to get to you and the child you're carrying. Whether or not Alexon has your best interests at heart is yet to be seen. We need proof."

Well, that was a start. "And what do we do in the meanwhile?"

He searched her face, and her pulse reacted to the concern she saw in his eyes.

"We get you someplace safe from danger for a while. You need to rest. I'd also feel better if we had a doctor check you out, to make sure you're okay. You have been through a lot and—"

"I'm fine." She couldn't prevent a tiny smile. "But thanks for caring."

He frowned. "Scout, how could you—"

She shook her head, cutting off whatever he would have said next. This was becoming too intense. She wasn't prepared to handle that. "Let's leave it at that, okay?"

He nodded once, reluctantly. She couldn't bear to hear him say what she'd feared he might. If he did she would never be able to hold on to what little objectivity she had left. Her baby's life depended on her ability to think clearly. She couldn't let anything—not even Max—cloud the issues.

"How do you propose we get out of here without being followed?" she asked, moving on to the next matter at hand.

Max grinned. The unexpectedness, the sheer sexiness and beauty of it took her breath away.

"You'd be surprised what we Colby agents can do," he teased.

SCOUT FINGERED HER LOCKET as she watched the parking lot from the window in Max's office. He'd explained to her that it was perfectly safe, since they were on the fourth floor and the windows were protected by a dark tint. The screening allowed those inside to see out, but anyone outside couldn't see in, nor could harsh UV rays of the sun penetrate the shield.

Simon Ruhl, wearing Max's clothes and a baseball cap, and another member of the Colby staff, Nicole Reed Michaels, who wore Scout's clothes and a large floppy hat to conceal her hair, walked across the parking lot and climbed into Max's SUV. Scout watched, expecting to see an unidentified vehicle fall in behind them as they exited the parking lot. But nothing else moved. Ian Michaels, Nicole's husband and Victoria Colby's second in command, and another of Max's co-workers, Ryan Braxton, were to follow Max's SUV, but Max had told her she would not see them leave the parking lot. Ian Michaels was too good to get caught.

Max had also warned her not to expect to see the tail. If anyone waited out there, it would likely be someone highly trained in the art of surveillance. They wouldn't simply drive out after their prey.

"You ready?" he asked from right behind her.

Scout could feel his body heat; he stood so close. She fought the urge to lean into him and allow him to support her with all that strength she could feel emanating from him. But that would be a mistake. She had to stay focused. And so did he. They were both professionals. Each knew the deal and had accepted by unspoken mutual consent to meet those terms.

"Let's do it." She turned to face him, and he immediately moved back a step, giving her space.

He hesitated a moment, as if held captive by the pull of attraction—the same attraction playing havoc with her equilibrium—before turning to lead the way to their planned escape route.

Scout followed Max down the long corridor, trying hard not to stare at the breadth of his shoulders or at the way he moved. Her heart fluttered and she couldn't help but grin at the suave picture he made in Simon Ruhl's dark suit. Of course, she didn't look half-bad in Nicole Reed's navy designer slacks and white silk blouse. Nicole was about an inch taller, but otherwise the size was nearly perfect.

Max greeted members of the staff as he met one after another arriving for work. He didn't slow to introduce anyone to Scout because they were on a time clock here. They couldn't risk waiting too long, giving the tail too much opportunity to discover he'd been had.

"Good morning, Max," an elegant, feminine voice said from somewhere beyond him.

Scout leaned to the left to see who'd spoken. The

woman was of medium height and impeccably dressed. Her hair was dark and peppered with gray. Scout decided she was maybe fifty and definitely the boss.

"Good morning, Victoria."

"And you must be Scout Jackson," the woman said as Max stepped aside and turned slightly toward her. He started to introduce them, but Victoria didn't give him the chance. "I'm Victoria Colby."

Scout nodded and extended her hand. "It's a pleasure to meet you, ma'am."

Victoria closed both hands over Scout's and shook it firmly, then said, "I'm so sorry about your uncle. And I'm also certain he would want me to do whatever it takes to help you. Let me assure you that we intend to do just that."

Scout wanted to believe that Victoria Colby's statement was nothing more than political rhetoric, but that wasn't the case. Her words were spoken sincerely and the look in her eyes backed them up. Maybe Alexon had hired this firm, but Scout had a feeling the Colby Agency focused on truth and justice more than beefing up its bank account.

"Thank you. I appreciate your support."

Victoria turned to Max then. "Be careful, Max."

Scout wondered as she and Max boarded the elevator what gave a woman like Victoria Colby the strength and stamina to oversee this kind of operation. Scout loved her P.I. business down in Houston, but it was nothing compared to this. She couldn't imagine the depth of devotion it took to reach this level. Victoria Colby had to be one special lady.

Max led Scout to a first-floor exit on the opposite side of the building from the parking lot. Simon

Ruhl's SUV was parked near the curb, waiting for them.

Max quickly ushered Scout into the passenger seat and rounded the hood to climb behind the wheel. The sooner they were out of here the less likely they were to be spotted by anyone hanging around to keep an eye on the agency.

"Do you think we're clear?" Scout asked, reading his mind far too accurately.

Max started the vehicle and eased out onto the street. "There's always the chance they'd expect a decoy. That's why we're going to take the scenic route to our destination."

When her safety belt was snapped into place, Scout relaxed in the luxurious leather seat. "Where exactly is our destination?"

Max divided his attention between the street and the rearview mirror, keeping an eye out for a tail. "A guest house owned by the Colby Agency."

At her questioning look, he added, "It's for out of town guests. Friends of Victoria's. You know." He shrugged. "Security's top-notch. You'll like it."

She seemed satisfied for the time being with that answer. Max had been to the house before and he was certain she would like it. Nestled on a secluded lakefront property, the house looked more like a Malibu beach house than a Chicago getaway. The property was enclosed by a high security wall with a gated entrance. And the house itself—well, it was every bit as sophisticated and elegant as the lady who owned it. Victoria Colby had very discriminating taste.

The reappearance of a white van in the rearview mirror pushed Max to a higher state of alert. The van had pulled in behind him three blocks ago, then turned off. Now it was back. Though there appeared to be no distinctive markings, he was pretty sure it was the same vehicle.

"We may have trouble," he told Scout, keeping most of his attention on the vehicle in his rearview mirror.

She swore and drew her nine-millimeter from the purse Nicole had provided.

"Let's stay cool for a couple more blocks," Max suggested. It was 8:50 on a Wednesday morning in downtown Chicago. Any number of companies used these same nondescript vans. The driver had made no moves of aggression just yet.

"How can we protect ourselves with all these people around?" She surveyed the pedestrians on the sidewalks hurrying to their places of employment.

"There you go, reading my mind again," Max mused aloud as he took a right at the next light. Maybe it was because they were in the same line of work...or maybe it simply was. Whatever the case, she thought entirely too much like he did. That was a little scary.

Several turns and long minutes later, the white van was still behind them. Max swore softly. Time to put some asphalt between them. Nearing the outskirts of downtown, he gunned the engine and headed for an area that was not likely to be crowded this early in the morning, and would prove difficult maneuvering to a driver unfamiliar with the streets.

The first crack of glass had Max pressing more firmly on the accelerator. Simon would not be happy that his driver's-side mirror was shattered. Max responded with a sudden left turn.

Scout twisted in her seat, simultaneously lowering the window and preparing to take a shot.

"Keep your head down," Max roared as he took a quick, hard right.

"Can't return fire with my head down," Scout argued as she squeezed off a couple of shots. The van swerved, but didn't slow in its pursuit.

His heart hammering into warp speed, Max tried another evasive maneuver in hopes of putting distance between them. The van never let up, staying right behind them.

Three consecutive shots struck the SUV. Scout cried out in pain after the last one. Blood bloomed on the sleeve of her borrowed white blouse.

"Get down!" Max ordered. A mixture of fear and fury took over and he stomped even harder on the accelerator, propelling the SUV forward. He took the necessary turns and headed back toward the loop, the van right behind him, the driver still pulling off the occasional shot.

Scout hunched low in her seat, struggling to stop the flow of blood spilling down her right arm.

Max clenched his jaw hard and focused on driving. He didn't have any more time to try and lose this tail. There was only one way to be rid of it: he drove straight down Michigan Avenue at top speed.

The sound of sirens wailing did the trick.

The van made an abrupt turn and sped away. Conversely, Max stopped the SUV in the middle of the street and slammed the gearshift into Park.

"We'll get you to a hospital," he said to Scout,

his words strained with the tension rocketing through him. "Let me help you with that."

Before he could attempt to help, the driver's side door was jerked open and the barrel of a weapon leveled on him. "Get out of the car, sir!" the cop commanded.

Raising his arms above his head, Max did as he was instructed. It would only take a few minutes to straighten out the situation, since Victoria Colby was an honorary member of the Chicago Police Department. Right now all that mattered was that the cop on Scout's side of the vehicle was already calling for EMT support.

Scout's gray eyes, fraught with fear and pain, stared directly into his as the officer patted him down. In that split second Max made her a promise with his own eyes: everything was going to be fine. He would see to it.

MAX PACED THE CORRIDOR outside the examining room where Scout was being treated. Victoria had taken care of the situation with the police, and a detective had driven Max straight to the hospital where Scout had already been taken. The detective had finished taking Max's statement there, then had left to add one more open investigation to the pile no doubt already cluttering his desk. Ian and Simon had driven over, to make sure that Max and Scout were all right. They'd left Max's SUV in the emergency area parking lot. Simon didn't ask what condition his own SUV was in, and Max was too worried about Scout to mention it. Thinking back now, he was pretty sure the vehicle was riddled with at least a dozen bullet holes. He doubted Simon would be so quick to lend his car again.

At the moment the only thing Max could think about was Scout and the baby. He was relatively sure the injury wasn't life threatening. There had been a lot of blood, but that was to be expected. She'd looked calm enough. She'd walked to the ambulance under her own steam. But she'd also looked extremely pale and vulnerable. His gut tied up in knots at the memory.

He was supposed to protect her. Had sworn he would. And look at the mess he'd made.

Max plunged his fingers through his hair and closed his eyes, ordering himself to stay calm. The last thing she needed was to see him in this condition. Some protector he was.

He had to pull himself together.

SCOUT SAT ON THE EDGE of the treatment table and tried not to flinch as the doctor finished suturing her wound. It wasn't so bad. Just an ugly tear through skin and muscle. After the stitches healed she'd be as good as new. She trembled, and railed at herself for doing so.

She was fine.

The baby was fine.

But that had been too close.

What if she'd been injured badly enough to lose the baby?

What if Max had been killed?

She closed her eyes and ordered herself to suck it up. She was stronger than this. She knew she was. Her life would never be her own—her child would never be safe—if she didn't see this through.

She should tell Max the truth. What if he'd died today, not knowing that the child she carried was his? She would regret that decision for the rest of her life. She'd been wrong in not telling him.

He had the right to know.

She had to come clean with him. She owed him that. She owed it to the baby growing inside her.

A nurse entered the room with Max right behind her.

"Look who I found pacing outside," she said cheerily. "Your husband was worried sick about you." The nurse patted Scout on the leg. "I told him he could just come on in and hold your hand."

Husband.

The nurse didn't know, of course, that Max wasn't her husband. But he was the father of her child.

Scout's gaze connected with his, and every ounce of courage she had summoned just minutes ago scattered for parts unknown. The worry she saw in those blue eyes, the vulnerable state in which the encounter had left him, evidently rendered him incapable of hiding his emotions. The depth of his feelings for her was right there in his eyes.

And she'd let him believe a lie.

Would he ever forgive her?

Dear God…was she brave enough to risk that he wouldn't?

Chapter Ten

Small waves lapping against the shoreline made Scout want to sit on the dock and hang her feet in the cool, refreshing water. Trees bursting with autumn color—deep russets and flaming oranges—hugged the property like a protective barrier spawned by nature. A security wall at least twelve feet in height snaked among them, surrounding the lavishly landscaped lawn.

Just when Scout was sure she couldn't be dazzled any further, they entered the massive, contemporary-style house and she was awestruck all over again.

"Wow," she said with a sigh. "This is…" she shook her head "…amazing." Even that didn't describe it. She felt certain one word would never be sufficient to accurately describe this mansion.

"*Spectacular* is the word I think you're looking for," Max offered, looking every bit as awestruck as she felt. He dropped her duffel onto the floor. "Truly spectacular. No matter how many times I come here, I'm always startled all over again."

Scout moved deeper into the two-story foyer, her sneakers rasping softly on the marble floor. She heard the telltale beeps of Max entering in the security code. This place was like a fortress. Surely they would be safe here.

Come to think of it, she mused as she turned around slowly in the center of the room, she could get used to a place like this.

To her surprise, her stomach, still queasy from the discomfort of the stitches and the medicinal smell of the hospital, rumbled hungrily. She'd been sure when she left the emergency room that she might never eat again.

"Is there a restaurant somewhere around here?" she asked hopefully, biting her lip. She was suddenly ravenous.

Max moved toward her, his hands tucked into the pockets of his borrowed suit trousers, his pale blue shirt open at the throat and stained with her blood, his tanned jaw sporting golden stubble. He looked far too dangerously sexy for his own good—or hers.

"I'm afraid going to a restaurant would be too risky," he said solemnly as he stopped a few feet away. "However, the kitchen here will be well-stocked. Victoria sent someone over to take care of it as soon as the decision was made to come here. Are you hungry?"

She nodded, but the hunger she'd experienced seconds ago had unexpectedly morphed into another kind. Her mind immediately conjured the remembered taste of his lips and the feel of his muscled body beneath her exploring palms. She recalled the way he'd looked at her in that treatment room, and her knees felt weak all over again.

Could she have been so wrong all these months? Had their time together affected him as much as it had her? Why hadn't he called? Or…or something?

"I'm starved," she blurted, certain if she didn't get back on track she would say something she'd regret. Her latest epiphany had nothing to do with the reality of the situation. This was too important to let personal feelings get in the way. Her baby's life depended on what they did. She immediately suppressed the guilt that rose at how she'd kept the truth from Max. She couldn't deal with that right now, either.

"This way."

She followed him through the house, barely keeping up, she was so mesmerized by the beauty of the decor and furnishings. The artwork was also spectacular. Everything was perfect. Only a professional could have decorated a house so precisely and exquisitely down to the very smallest detail.

"Has anyone ever lived here or was this place built as a retreat for friends and associates of your boss?" she asked, then forgot all about the question. "Oh, my God," she muttered. The kitchen was huge, as big as her whole apartment back home, with beautiful mahogany cabinets and marble countertops. The view over the lake from the large picture window was breathtaking.

"It's just a kitchen," Max teased, then, as he peered into the commercial-size stainless steel refrigerator, suggested, "How about a salad?"

"Fine." She was too distracted by her surroundings to care what she ate. The brass rack that hung over the enormous center island held dried spices and sparking copper pots and pans. Scout stared at everything, taking in the lavish details.

"This house was once Victoria's home," Max said in answer to her question.

Scout hopped onto one of the stools flanking the island and folded her arms over her middle, only then remembering that she wore the matching jacket to the trousers Max had borrowed. The white blouse she'd been wearing had been cut into pieces and removed by the nurse. Max had given her the jacket, which, other than being too large, looked pretty good with the navy slacks Nicole had lent her. Now, however, both ensembles were basically trashed.

Max busied himself with making the salads. Scout simply enjoyed the view—of him, mostly. He really did look like a beach hunk from some California shore. She recalled well how tanned and rippled his body was. Warmth pooled deep inside her at the memory. A smile curved her lips. She hadn't thought about sex in a while and she'd purposely kept Max out of her fantasies as much as possible. Which wasn't nearly enough.

"Let's sit over here." He carried their plates to the breakfast nook nestled in a huge bay window. "What would you like to drink? There's cola and juice."

She wondered briefly if he had told whoever had come to stock the kitchen that she was pregnant and would need something to drink other than wine. This place definitely looked like a "wine" kind of place.

"Juice, please."

He nodded and crossed the room to fill her order. Minutes later he returned with two glasses of grape juice. Scout's mouth watered just looking at it. She loved grape juice. Had craved it like candy for the past two months of her pregnancy.

"So, why doesn't Victoria live here now?" she asked between bites.

Max studied his salad for so long that Scout wasn't sure whether he intended to answer her or if he'd lost the thread of the conversation. Then he said, "This is where she lived with her husband and son." When his gaze returned to Scout's she knew the rest was not good.

"Her son went missing while they lived here, and was never found." He cleared his throat and straightened in his chair. "Her husband was murdered a few years later."

Heavy silence fell over the room for a while and Scout shuddered at the prospect of how horrifying it must be to lose a child and a husband. She couldn't imagine the pain and suffering. The respect she already had for Victoria Colby tripled and then some. That she could suffer such loss and still carry on with her life, still manage such a high-profile agency… It went beyond Scout's ability to comprehend the kind of courage and determination the lady must possess.

"Anyway," Max added, breaking the awkward tension, "she never comes back here. Using it as a guest house is better than letting it go to waste."

Scout considered her own crisp greens, but instead of taking a bite, asked, "Why doesn't she just sell it? Get rid of the memories altogether."

Those blue eyes, the color of the sea, looked directly into hers. "Her son was only seven when he was taken. Some people say that when an abducted child grows up—assuming he isn't murdered—he sometimes finds his way back home to wherever he lived before." Max cleared his throat again. Scout knew he was struggling with the same emotion choking off her own ability to speak. "That's why she keeps it…in case he ever comes back."

The silence surrounded them again. Emotions thickened. Scout forced herself to eat the salad, knowing the child growing inside her needed nourishment.

In that moment, sitting in the elegant kitchen in Victoria Colby's former home, Scout realized all the things she hadn't considered since discovering she was pregnant.

She hadn't stopped to ask herself what she would do with her child when she was gone on a case. She hadn't wondered how she would handle him or her being sick, as children often were, with no one to fill in for her at the office. There was no other income except hers. What had she been thinking when she'd presumed she could do this alone?

She stole a covert look at Max. He'd finished his lunch and was staring at the plate as if there was something else he wanted to say. Or maybe he was still hungry and couldn't decide if he intended to do anything about it. Should she tell him now? Just come out with it and let the chips fall where they may?

"Max—"

"Scout—"

They both stopped abruptly and looked at one another expectantly.

"Go ahead," he offered with a wave of his hand.

She shook her head. "No, you go first."

He stared at the glass tabletop again for what felt like forever before lifting his gaze to hers. "I tried to call." He shrugged. "You know, afterward. But you never phoned back."

He'd called? "I didn't get any messages."

"I left two," he insisted. "A few days, maybe a week after they released us."

She frowned, trying to figure out why she hadn't gotten the messages. Then it dawned on her. "Someone broke into my house right after I got back home. I suppose it could have been a week," she said, not realizing until after the words were uttered that they didn't really explain anything. "They took my TV, VCR, telephone answering system and new CD player."

"So you didn't know I'd called." He looked even more confused now...or maybe just uncertain of what he should say next.

"No. I didn't. I thought you..." Oh, Lord, she didn't want to tell him that she'd thought he wasn't interested. Then he'd know she had been...still was...

Silence enveloped them once more, while they looked deep into each other's eyes and wondered what might have been.

Did this mean there was hope? Anticipation churned through her. God, she didn't want to get her heart broken by this man all over again. But if there was any possibility...

Max searched for the right words to say, but he wasn't sure there were any. She hadn't returned his calls because she hadn't gotten the messages. To say that he was relieved would have been putting it mildly. He'd been almost certain she felt something for him. He'd been positive of it when he'd held her in his arms. But after they'd been released and she'd returned to Houston, time and distance had made him uncertain. Fate had thrown them back together, given them a second chance. Well, maybe that was pushing it. This might not mean anything, and he wasn't prepared to skate that far out on thin ice until he was more certain of her feelings than he was now.

She stood, picked up her plate and glass and gave him a weary smile. "I know it's only two o'clock, but I think I'll go take a shower and a nap." She hesitated a moment. "That is, if you think it's safe enough to let my guard down."

"You do that. Pick any room you'd like. I'll keep watch. We're safe here."

He watched her go, wishing not for the first time that he could go with her. But she still had major issues to sort out. Such as how she felt about the man who'd fathered her child. Fury knotted Max's insides every time he thought of the guy. And there was the Alexon business. Until all that was cleared up, they both had only one choice, and that was to keep this thing between them strictly business.

BY THE TIME SCOUT EMERGED from the shower, Max had delivered her duffel to her chosen room. She'd picked what looked to be the master suite, which was enormous and absolutely beautiful. She could definitely see Victoria Colby in this room. It fit the woman's sophisticated style and personality.

Scout took her time drying her hair, checking carefully to see that she hadn't gotten her bandage wet, then slipping on a clean T-shirt and climbing into the massive bed. She moaned with delight as she sank beneath the luxurious covers. If she'd ever slept in a bed this heavenly she had no recollection, and she was certain she would never have forgotten the experience.

She chastised herself again for not telling Max the truth when she'd had the chance. When he'd said he had called her, a new kind of hope had bloomed. His revelation, combined with what she'd seen in his eyes at the hospital, made her wonder if his feelings for her went deeper than she'd first thought. Was there any chance they could have a relationship? She wanted it desperately.

With that in mind, she'd kept her secret to herself.

It sounded selfish, she knew, but she had to see where this possible relationship might go. She wanted Max to want her for herself, not for the baby. She had to make sure that what he felt for her was enough on its own merit without the added motivation of having a child on the way. What good was a future with Max if it was based on her pregnancy rather than on love?

Maybe it really was selfish of her, but she wanted it all. She wanted him to love her the way she'd dreamed during all those lonely nights since they'd been released from isolation. She wanted to have him say the words to *her*. Then she could tell him the rest of the story.

Okay, maybe she was rationalizing. But she was very nearly certain it was the right thing to do. If he couldn't love her completely, then the marriage would never work in the long run. She'd seen too many fall apart—firsthand. She was always following husbands and wives around, hired by their spouses to check on suspected cheaters. Marriage could be a bad business if the partners went into the arrangement without all their ducks in a row. Scout wanted to do this the right way, one duck neatly lined up behind the next.

WHEN SCOUT AWOKE it was completely dark in the room. For several seconds she lay utterly still, listening, searching her memory for time and place.

The Colby Agency guest house.

She'd lain down for a nap and had fallen asleep. Glancing at the bedside clock as she got up, she realized that it was almost eight o'clock. Wow, she had slept the afternoon away. But she'd needed the rest. Her hand went automatically to her tummy and she smiled. Soon she would be able to feel the baby moving inside her. She couldn't wait. Briefly, she wondered if it was a boy or a girl.

Her eyes widened. What on earth was she going to name this kid? The image of Max flitted through her awareness. He would have some say in that, she supposed. Unless he turned his back on her for lying to him. He might turn on her…but he would never turn on his child.

Still, she refused to think about that right now. She straightened her T-shirt, pulled on a pair of jeans from her duffel bag and made a quick trip to the bathroom before going downstairs. Already she was hungry again. She shook her head. If she wasn't throwing up she was devouring anything in sight. Again, her mind immediately presented the likeness of Max. Boy, even pregnant she had a dirty mind.

The upstairs hall was dimly lit by lovely seashell wall sconces that allowed her to make her way to the landing and the stairs without any trouble.

The staircase swept along one wall, curving downward with such grace and elegance that it took her breath all over again. The crystal chandelier that hung from the soaring ceiling sent shards of light spilling across the marble. As beautiful as the house was, Scout was shrouded in sadness once more as she thought of the tragedies that had befallen the woman who owned it.

The marble of the foyer floor felt cool beneath her bare feet as Scout crossed to the living room or whatever rich folks called the huge space. She figured Max might be there, since she could hear the low sounds of a television.

When she stepped into the enormous room, her breath stalled in her lungs. A dark-haired man stood in front of the sofa, facing the doorway she had just entered, as if he'd heard her approach. Which was impossible, of course, since she'd been barefoot and completely silent.

Recognition jarred her heart back to an acceptable rhythm. "Mr. Cooper...Doug," she said, with a flood of relief.

He smiled, that charming expression that would make any woman swoon. Her hand went of its own volition to her chest. "Good evening, Miss Jackson." He relaxed visibly. She realized then that he'd been prepared to draw his weapon.

She moistened her lips and produced a smile. "How's Donna?" Donna England was her assistant. She could just imagine how Donna had enjoyed keeping company with this guy. The woman, who was as much friend as co-worker, had no doubt kept Douglas Cooper on his toes trying to keep things strictly business.

"Miss England is quite...well," he said, his tone the only evidence she needed to know that Donna had likely cornered him in the office the very first day they'd met.

"When did you get here?" Scout decided she could use some more of that juice and… "Where's Max?" she asked abruptly. If he'd run out on her and decided to make a move without her she was going to—

"I talked him into getting some shut-eye while you were resting." Doug lifted those broad shoulders in a careless shrug. "He resisted, of course, but I persuaded him."

Men, she mused. They always had to play it tough, especially if another man was around. "I'm glad. I think I'll get something to eat." She backed up a step. "You hungry?"

He skirted the end of the couch. "Coffee would be nice. Do you mind if I join you?"

"I'd be offended if you didn't."

That smile again. It was nothing short of a miracle that Donna had let him leave Houston. And thinking of home, Scout realized she should check in with her office. Find out firsthand what was going on, and get the lowdown on Mr. *GQ* here.

She hunted through the refrigerator until she found the makings of a sandwich, which she promptly threw together and consumed, almost groaning in satisfaction. When had eating become such a pleasure? If she continued on this course she'd be huge by the time the baby came.

Doug sipped his coffee, seeming to enjoy watching her eat like the proverbial pig.

"I don't usually devour food like this," she felt obliged to say. No woman in her right mind wanted a guy like him to think she gorged frequently.

"I like a woman with a healthy appetite," Doug assured her. "They usually have character that's lacking in their more finicky counterparts."

Scout pushed her empty plate aside and relaxed more fully in her chair. "Answer a question for me, Doug."

"And what would that be?" He looked amused, but not condescending. He appeared to thoroughly enjoy conversing with the opposite sex.

She hoped he was ready for her. Under normal circumstances she was very straightforward, preferring the truth over niceties. "What's a rich guy like you doing playing P.I.?"

He considered her question for a time, his good-natured expression never changing. If her bluntness annoyed him, he didn't show it.

"No offense, mind you," she added quickly. "I mean, I'm sure you're very good at your job. I'm just curious."

"None taken," he replied promptly. "Max told you?"

She almost laughed, but stifled it just in time. "Max didn't have to tell me anything. It's in your breeding, dear boy." She did laugh then, but just a little. "It's the way you speak, the way you dress and carry yourself. Very nice, don't get me wrong, but unmistakable."

He frowned briefly, then leveled a frank gaze on her. "I wanted to do more. Risking people's money for your livelihood isn't quite so stimulating as risking your life for people. I do prefer, however, to keep my background out of the equation."

She nodded, knowing exactly what he meant even if she would have put it a little differently. "I understand.'' She stood and cleared her dishes from the table. She wanted to check on Max and, if he was awake, find out what he had planned for their next step.

Before she left the kitchen, she paused next to Doug's chair and put a reassuring hand on his shoulder. ''Do yourself a favor,'' she suggested. ''If you really want to keep your background a secret, get rid of the Rolex and buy your clothes off the rack in a department store.'' She smiled at his surprised expression, then patted that broad shoulder. ''And stop being so polite. Tough guys aren't supposed to be quite so polished.''

She left Doug to make what he would of that, and padded back up the stairs. She looked first right, then left. There had to be seven or eight rooms up here. Max could be in any one of them. Might as well start on her right, she decided.

It turned out he had selected the room right across the hall from hers. She should have suspected as much; he wouldn't want to be far away. The door was open so she paused there and squinted into the darkness, trying to make out his form. He lay on the bed; that much she could tell.

When she would have stepped into the shadowy room, he spoke, ''Is something wrong?'' The lamp on the bedside table came on and he sat up.

She swallowed the unexpected lump that welled in her throat as her eyes took in his bare chest. He'd removed the bloodstained shirt, but he still wore the trousers. Acres of tanned, rippled flesh held her captivated for a beat too long.

''Nothing's wrong.'' She moved toward the bed, utilizing every fiber of courage she possessed to make the journey and then sit down next to him while still maintaining her appearance of calm. "I wanted to talk to you about what we're going to do next." She'd had time to rest, and her mind was churning with possibilities. If the lab analysis of the documents they'd found in her uncle Harold's house didn't match any of the Alexon correspondence, they needed to take other measures to prove her accusations against them.

Max looked at her and she shivered. Dammit, she tried not to, but she just couldn't help it. His hair was tousled from sleep and his jaw still glittered with golden stubble. She wanted to touch him almost more than she wanted to take her next breath.

"I've decided to confront Alexon," he stated.

Her eyes rounded with disbelief. "But what if—"

"No ifs. When I confront them face-to-face, I'll get a reaction. I need to analyze that reaction. Then I'll know."

She knew what he meant.

Then he would know if Alexon officials were lying…or if she was.

Chapter Eleven

Max watched Scout roam the great room like a caged tiger the next morning. Though impatient and furious, her movements were every bit as fluid and exotic. She didn't like his plan and was making no bones about it.

"What do you expect them to tell you?" she argued. "They'll only use the opportunity to have their people follow you right back to me." She shoved a handful of hair behind one ear and crossed her arms over her chest. "I think you should rethink your strategy."

Despite her blatant rebuke and lack of faith, he had to smile. There was something about the way she tilted her head when she was angry that got to him. Something about the determined set of her shoulders, the way she pushed her hair aside or shot daggers at him with those smoky-gray eyes.

"There's nothing amusing about this," she snapped, apparently noting his unintended smile. She looked to Cooper then. "What do you think?"

Max stood braced in the open doorway, too edgy to sit. In contrast, Cooper lounged on the sofa, looking completely relaxed and at the same time fully prepared. Truth was, Max needed the distance. When Scout had visited him in his room last night, it had been all he could do not to touch her, take her into his arms and hold her the way he longed to.

He'd sworn this morning that he would do a better job of hanging on to his perspective. She didn't make it easy, but he would do his damnedest.

"I think it's the only choice we have," Cooper finally said, agreeing with Max's strategy. He stopped Scout's argument with an uplifted hand. "Hear me out." She huffed in frustration, but listened. "We're at an impasse here. We need a re-action."

She stared at the floor for a long moment, anxiety making her posture rigid.

"I will not lead them back here," Max vowed. "That I can promise you."

She started to pace again, the fingers of her right hand going immediately to the locket she always wore. He'd wondered about that. Even when they'd gone into isolation she'd reach for it, but the necklace had soon been confiscated along with the rest of their personal belongings. She'd gotten it back in the end and had seemed happier about that than about being released.

She stopped abruptly and looked at him across the expanse of the room. Those gray eyes had darkened to the color of cold, hard steel. "All right. I want this over with."

She walked out of the room, not even sparing him another glance.

Max closed his eyes and shook his head. What did he have to do to prove his loyalty to the woman?

Yes, Alexon had hired the Colby Agency, but Max's first loyalty was to the truth and the integrity of the agency. If Alexon was up to no good, they would not get away with using the Colby group.

"Do what you have to." Cooper stood and moved toward the door, his expression far too knowing. "I'll talk to her. Don't worry, she'll be okay."

Max tensed. His own conviction that this was far too personal was one thing; having one of his co-workers recognize that fact was another thing entirely. "I know she'll be fine. Is there something else you wanted to imply?"

Cooper smiled. "I'm not implying anything." He started to walk out of the room again, then hesitated. "Actions speak louder than words, my friend."

Max blew out a disgusted breath as Cooper strolled away, heading toward the kitchen for more coffee, most likely. Max had foregone breakfast—even his usual coffee—this morning. He'd felt ill the moment he awoke. The idea of drinking or eating anything had made his stomach churn violently. He'd been lucky in the past, had never once gotten sick on the job. This latest caper appeared to have jinxed him, marking a definite end to his lucky streak.

He glanced at his watch and then took the stairs at a run. An impromptu visit to Alexon was the first thing on his agenda; no point in wasting any more time. Still, he couldn't leave without assuring Scout once more that he would keep her covered.

The door to the master suite was closed. Max rapped lightly on it. "Scout, I need to talk to you before I go."

To his surprise the door opened immediately, as

if she'd been waiting for him. "What?" She leaned against the doorjamb, annoyance still clear in her expression. "You've made up your mind. What else is there to say?"

He watched her lips move as she spoke, and he had the sudden, unbidden, almost overpowering urge to kiss her. The fact that she was carrying another man's child didn't seem to matter. He only wanted to take that sweet face into both hands and kiss her until she kissed him back. Apparently, he wasn't sick enough for his libido to slow down where she was concerned.

Time out, he ordered his wayward thoughts.

He had to at least attempt to keep this impersonal.

"They won't know where you are until I'm convinced it's safe." That smoky gaze collided with his and he added, "You have my word." For one long moment they gazed at each other, didn't even breathe…just looked. Finally, when he could bear the tension no longer, he managed to say, "I'll be back soon."

He left her without a backward glance. If he had he was certain he would have rushed back to her and kissed her in spite of logic and reasoning. The need had been so strong, the desire so clear, not only in him, but in her, as well. But he couldn't cross that line.

This was a case. This was business….

And the last thing he wanted was to get involved with Scout again when she was on the rebound. They'd been down that road before. She'd been engaged to Kimble, was now carrying his child. Max would be crazy to pretend she couldn't possibly feel anything for her old lover.

Would things have been different if she'd gotten his messages? Would that be his child she carried? Was she really certain it wasn't? Was *he?* He released a weary breath. Wishful thinking....

Max forced the troubling thoughts away. The past was a done deal. The sooner he got to the bottom of the Alexon situation, the sooner he and Scout could settle this thing between them once and for all.

REGIS BRANDON WAS NOT happy with Max's announcement that he would not reveal Scout's location until he was certain it was safe to do so.

"My company hired your agency to do a job," Brandon said hotly, failing miserably in his efforts to keep his voice low so that other diners wouldn't note the tension at their table. He'd insisted that Max have lunch with him away from the Alexon facility.

Max had his own ideas about why the meeting had been moved off-site. Brandon wanted to create an atmosphere of congeniality and intimacy, as if he and Max were longtime friends. Too bad his plan had the opposite effect.

"You're absolutely correct," Max allowed. "And we will gladly perform that service as long as it does not infringe on another human being's rights. I need to feel confident that Miss Jackson's accusations are unfounded. Can you give me that assurance?"

The executive had been weaving around the subject for the last hour. Max had an uneasy feeling that he was not only avoiding the issue, but was hiding something pertinent to the matter, as well.

Brandon sighed deeply, but somehow managed to retain his composure. Max could see that he was

madder than hell, but determined to keep up a fa-
cade of casualness. The CEO of a major research
facility apparently didn't want to cause a scene in
his favorite ritzy restaurant. Max had no sympathy
for him whatsoever; after all, he had chosen the
meeting place.

"All right," Brandon said at last. "The trouble
Miss Jackson has is not with us. Our only concern
is her safety." He glanced covertly from right to left,
then leveled his gaze on Max. "If Biogenisis gets
their hands on her first, there's no telling what they
will do. You don't know what those fiends are capable of. She, as well as the child, would be in grave
danger. The folks at Biogenisis have no scruples.
They want the antidote at any cost." He leaned
slightly forward. "Do you understand what I'm saying here, Maxwell? They would do anything to have
it. *Anything.*"

Max narrowed his eyes, studying the man carefully. "Who is behind Biogenisis?" He'd never
heard of them, but that didn't mean anything. His
only knowledge of the medical research industry involved corporations who were clients of the Colby
Agency.

"The CEO, Winston Ames, once oversaw
Alexon. Ames was tossed out on his ear when the
government discovered he had created K-141."

Now things were getting interesting. "What do
you mean? I thought K-141 was commissioned by
the Defense Department."

Brandon shook his head. "Ames did that on his
own. It's illegal, you know, to create something like
that for the sole purpose of auctioning it off to the
highest bidder."

The tension simmering inside Max escalated. "So why is Alexon involved in the matter at all?"

Brandon sighed again. "Alexon's board felt responsible for what Ames had done so they made it their mission to undo the damage. To find the antidote, thus clearing their record."

The first inklings of fear joined the tension mushrooming inside Max. Alexon and Biogenisis were in a secret war, and Scout was caught right in the middle. A conflict of this magnitude threatened national security. The United States government had to be deeply involved. But why hadn't a government agency stepped in to seize control of the situation?

Because Alexon was covering it up.

Damn.

Scout was in more trouble than she knew.

Brandon leaned forward again. "The fetus she carries is the key to the antidote."

And Scout was right. They wanted her child.

Max stared straight into Brandon's eyes and said coldly, "The baby is not negotiable."

Brandon was shorter and about fifty pounds lighter than Max. He looked to be forty years old, and not particularly fit. But though Max was now glaring at him with murder in his eyes, the man didn't even flinch.

"Oh, you misunderstand my intent," Brandon hastened to reply. "We're not trying to obtain the child. Quite the contrary. Our only interest is in the umbilical cord and the stem cells that it will contain."

Unconvinced, Max turned his intimidation tactics up a notch, leaning forward slightly, making Brandon squirm a little. "That's all you need to develop a corrected antidote?"

The executive nodded jerkily. "Of course, we realize that you and Miss Jackson have to discuss the situation and come to an agreement. But it's the right thing, the only thing to do. Your country's security rests on the decision."

He and Scout had a decision to make? Why did Brandon think Max had any say? As an advisor, maybe?

"Please assure Miss Jackson that our only concern right now is for her safety. If she is hurt and loses the child, our single most viable hope will be lost. She must know that we are sincerely concerned about her safety."

Max resumed his intimidating stare. "So you're admitting to holding her against her will?"

Brandon's eyes widened. "I'm...I'm not admitting to anything," he hedged, "other than attempting to ensure her safety. We at Alexon believe total isolation is the only assurance."

"What about Harold Atkins? Did you have him killed? Did he represent some threat to her?" Max pressed, firing off one probing question after another. He still wasn't convinced Alexon was behind the worst of this. Still, he had no intention of tipping his hand.

Brandon's expression closed instantly. "Harold was a trusted member of our staff. Head of our security. Why would Alexon have anything to do with his death?"

Max couldn't argue. The only way Alexon would have been responsible for Atkins's murder would have been if they had discovered him in the act of betrayal and had had no other choice to cover up the dirty business and keep it out of the press.

"The reason we called in the Colby Agency," Brandon added, "was because we knew Miss Jackson didn't trust us. We knew she would trust you."

Ha! If only they *really* knew, Max mused.

"I apologize for not being up front with you in the beginning," Brandon offered. "But you must see that we simply had to be careful."

"Why only Scout and the baby?" Max wanted to know. "Why not me? I'm immune to K-141."

Brandon sighed wearily. "The child's stem cells will be brimming with immunity much more so than you or Miss Jackson. It's our best chance at creating an effective antidote."

Max still had questions. "Why are we immune? What makes us special?"

"I can't answer that. We compared the two of you in every way possible, considered even the most remote factors you had in common. The only relevant conclusion was that you both spent a great deal of time in South America. And that may not be the answer, but we believe that's the connection."

Max nodded, pondering the possibility.

"Mr. Maxwell, we need those stem cells," Brandon urged.

"I'll have to discuss all this with Miss Jackson," Max allowed. "I can't promise you anything. But I will be in touch." He scooted back his chair, leaving the lunch he'd ordered untouched. His stomach still roiled at the very idea of eating.

"Please," Brandon said, making Max hesitate when he would have walked away, "don't let anything happen to her. I'm still not sure you understand how crucial her well-being is.''

"I understand all I need to."

Max walked away certain of only one thing—Scout's life was in grave danger.

SCOUT COULDN'T GET PAST the restlessness. She couldn't sit, she couldn't eat. She could only worry about Max and his confrontation with Alexon.

What if they killed him? She shuddered. He was too smart to walk into a trap. Still, there were so many of them. She touched the bandage on her arm. Anything could happen.

"How about I prepare some lunch?" Doug offered, breezing into the foyer. "I'm quite the chef, you know."

Scout smiled; she couldn't help herself. He was simply too charming to resist.

"Thanks, but I'm not hungry."

Doug scowled. "You should eat."

Before she could respond, a buzzer sounded, seeming to echo all around them.

"What's that?"

It didn't sound like any doorbell she'd ever heard. And it couldn't be Max; he'd have used the access code.

"Someone's at the gate," Doug explained. He moved to an intercom system near the front entry. "Yes."

"This is Dayco Delivery. I got a package for a Miss Jackson."

Doug looked questioningly at Scout. She shook her head and wondered if he was half as surprised as she was. Who knew they were here? As she walked over to join him, Doug made a couple more selections on the sophisticated-looking system, and the camera at the front gate sent an image to the six-inch monitor on the wall in front of them. A white panel van sporting a popular local carrier's logo was parked outside the gate. A man dressed in a proper uniform, holding a small package, stood next to it.

"Leave it at the gate. We'll pick it up later," Doug instructed.

"No can do," the driver countered. "Got to have a signature for this one."

Doug pointed to a button on the system's control panel. "Watch the monitor," he told Scout. "If anything happens that shouldn't, hit this panic button and hide until help arrives." He glanced down at her waist. "Where's your weapon?"

She reached under her T-shirt and removed the nine-millimeter from its resting place at the small of her back. "Right here."

"No heroics, Scout," he warned. "You do exactly as I told you."

She nodded. "Gotcha."

Scout watched the monitor, scarcely breathing. Who would send her a package? Who the hell would know where to send it? This had to be some kind of trick. Had Alexon forced her location out of Max already? Fear constricted her chest. Was he hurt? Or worse?

Doug didn't open the gate. The driver passed the clipboard between the wrought-iron bars and Doug did the same after he'd signed the delivery acceptance sheet. He then waited until the man had driven away before returning to the house.

Once Doug was back inside and had locked the

door behind him, Scout breathed a hell of a lot easier.

"Stay right there," he ordered.

She watched in confusion as he headed toward the rear deck with the small package in hand. She had to physically restrain herself from following him. He'd told her to stay here and she would; she wasn't taking any more risks. Her baby's life depended upon her staying healthy. She moved her sore arm. Yesterday had driven home all too well just how vulnerable she was.

The five minutes Doug was gone felt like fifty. Finally he returned, the package open in his hand. She realized then that he'd gone out back onto the deck, away from her, to open it just in case it was a bomb or some other booby trap.

"It's a cellular phone." He took the device out of the box and showed her. "I popped the housing open to be sure. No bugs, no explosives. Just a phone."

She took it from him and looked it over to see if she recognized it. She'd lost hers escaping from Alexon. She shook her head. "Who would send me—"

The phone in question rang and vibrated simultaneously. Scout almost dropped it, her heart surging into her throat. She swore and pressed her free hand to her chest. "That scared the hell out of me." It rang and vibrated again.

"Let me answer it." Doug took the phone from her and glanced at the caller ID before depressing the receive button. He shook his head, indicating the caller's ID wasn't displayed, and said, "Hello."

He listened for a second, then offered the phone to her. "It's for you."

Fear, as cold as ice, slid through her veins. She took the phone and pressed it to her ear. "Hello."

"Buttercup, it's Harold."

Shock paralyzed her. She couldn't speak. It was her uncle's voice. No one else ever called her by that nickname, not even her father.

"We have to meet. At my place. Come as soon as you can." The voice of her dead uncle added, "Don't let me down, Scout. I can explain everything."

The call was disconnected.

She lowered the phone and simply stared at it, unable to deal with the emotions whirling inside her.

"Who was it?" Doug took the phone from her hand and punched a few buttons. He shook his head. "The call log reads 'caller unknown.' It won't let me do a dial-back."

"This can't be," she mumbled.

Her knees buckled, and all that saved her from an up-close-and-personal encounter with the fancy Italian marble was Doug's swift reaction.

"Let's sit down," he suggested, supporting her entire weight in his capable arms. He lifted her effortlessly and carried her to the great room. After depositing her carefully on the sofa, he sat down on the table in front of her. "Who was it, Scout?"

She looked at him, knowing that she was glassy-eyed and on the verge of fainting. "It was my uncle. Harold Atkins."

If the news startled him he recovered too quickly for her to notice. "You know that's impossible."

She nodded. "I know." Her gaze locked with

Doug's. "But it was him." She shook her head and lifted a shoulder in an attempt at a shrug. "It was!"

MAX PAUSED AT THE GATE to the guest house and entered the access code. He drove through, then out of habit watched as the gates closed behind him. Parking his SUV near Doug's, he reviewed one last time all that Regis Brandon had said. Alexon's goal was to keep Scout, thus the baby, safe. Biogenisis was the real enemy—the ruthless ones who would go to any means to get access to the antidote.

Though he couldn't be certain, Max was ninety percent sure that Brandon was telling the truth about that part. Max had watched for signs of deception and found none. As the new CEO of Alexon, Brandon wanted to set to rights the mess the former man in charge had left. The whole story felt right to Max.

What gave him pause was Brandon's hedging toward the end of the conversation, as well as his comment that Max and Scout should discuss things and make a decision. Though Max considered himself wholly responsible for Scout's safety, whatever she decided regarding the baby was beyond his influence. He just couldn't fathom why Brandon thought he'd have some say in the matter. Maybe he figured that, since Max and Scout had been intimate, Max's opinion carried more weight than it did. Man, was he wrong.

Emerging from the vehicle, Max admitted that he and Scout had made some progress on a personal level. But neither of them could pursue it until the case was resolved. Still, he felt confident that she wanted, as he did, to explore the option of a relationship when this was over. She was pregnant with another man's child, but that didn't change what Max felt for her, not really. Except he had to tread cautiously here. She might choose to go back to the baby's father. The image of Gage Kimble abruptly loomed large in his mind and Max immediately squashed it. The case wasn't over. He couldn't dwell on the what-ifs of their personal lives until this situation was resolved.

He paused midway up the front steps and wondered for a moment if this odd calm about the baby was what his sister had felt when she'd married her husband. Her new stepdaughter had been four years old at the time, but Fiona had accepted the child without hesitation, as if she was her own. Other than the initial outrage at discovering Scout had been with another man since their time together—which was none of Max's business, since he'd had no hold on her anyway—he felt strangely at ease with the whole situation.

As soon as possible he intended to pursue this thing between them…if she was willing. He knew the connection to the baby's father would be strong under any circumstances. Max would simply have to learn to live with seeing the jerk from time to time.

Killing him wasn't an option.

A smile tugged at Max's lips. He had a plan. All he had to do now was see Scout safely through this uncertain period and get to the bottom of who had threatened her and her child.

Easier said than done, since he still had no proof of anything.

The door opened as Max reached it.

His instincts went immediately on point.

"We have a situation," Cooper said, his expression grim.

Max entered the foyer half expecting to find Scout missing. But that couldn't be the case. Doug would have informed him via his cellphone if things had gone that wrong.

When Cooper had locked up and reactivated the security system, he explained, "Scout received a package while you were out."

Confusion slammed into Max's brain, exacerbating the headache that had been nagging at him. "From whom?" No one had followed him, he was certain. Both he and Doug had pulled out all the stops, taken all the right precautions. *Impossible,* he thought, shaking his head in adamant denial. "No one outside the agency knows we're here."

Cooper spread his hands. "Someone does."

"What was it?" Max plowed a hand through his hair. Dammit. This would necessitate making another move. If their previous precautions hadn't foiled their pursuers, nothing would.

"A cellular phone. A few minutes after it was delivered, a call came in for Scout."

"What?"

Cooper nodded. "It gets even better," he added, knowing full well what Max must be thinking. "The caller was—"

"My uncle," Scout interrupted as she stepped into the foyer. "He needs me." She glanced at her watch. "It's time to go." She looked from Max to Cooper and back. "You're either with me or against me."

Chapter Twelve

He'd tried to reason with her. But Scout didn't want to listen to reason: she wanted answers.

A part of her wanted desperately to believe that somehow her uncle was alive and waiting for her at his house. She peered through the car window, staring at the darkness. At the fat raindrops sliding across the glass as Max drove through the night. She hadn't wanted to wait until dark, but Max would have it no other way.

Her uncle—the voice on the phone—hadn't given her a specific time. He'd just said that she needed to come as soon as she could.

Another part of her, the saner, more rational part, told her it wasn't possible. Her uncle was dead. She'd seen his murder with her own eyes. She'd visited his grave at the cemetery. Still, she hadn't looked closely at his supposedly fatal wound. She'd had to run for her life when the shot was fired. But she'd seen him fall, seen the blood. He was dead.

But the voice… It was him.

And no one, absolutely no one, used that old nickname. He'd dubbed her that when she was fourteen and taking riding lessons for the summer. Her father had been away on another of his secret missions, and she'd spent the long, hot summer with her uncle Harold in Texas. He'd insisted that a girl couldn't live in Texas and not know how to ride a horse. She had been thrilled with the lessons, but not with the nickname. Still, it had stuck. The only time he'd teased her with the nickname as an adult was once in a while when he called and was feeling especially sentimental. She always knew when he'd been reminiscing.

Who else could possibly know?

She shifted in the seat and stole a glance at Max. He didn't like this one bit. But he'd gone along when she'd sworn that she would find a way to ditch him if he didn't. The grim set of his profile in the dim glow of the dash lights told her he still wasn't happy.

Doug Cooper and Ryan Braxton followed a few car lengths behind. They planned to take an alternate route to her uncle's house once they reached the city. She and Max would approach by the usual route, Doug and Ryan from the rear, so to speak.

Not for the first time since the ordeal began, Scout said a quick, silent prayer. She'd never been afraid—not once in her entire life. Her father had called her fearless and had laughed when his special forces buddies suggested she should join up. But now safety was about more than just her own well-being. She had the baby to think of. But she had to do this. If there was even a remote chance her uncle was alive, she needed to help him. The only reason he would have faked his death would have been to fool Alexon or to bait her into a trap with the company. She frowned, forcing that thought away. Her uncle wouldn't hurt her, she knew. So if this was a trick, it had to have been engineered by Alexon.

Scout didn't care what Max thought; Regis Brandon was lying. His people had held her against her will. They were the ones trying to find her, to take her back into so-called protective custody. She knew what they wanted and she wasn't about to give it to them. But she couldn't prove any of it. She couldn't stop them without proof.

Still no one would take this baby from her.

Max eased the SUV over to the curb and shifted into Park. She sat up a little straighter. "We're not there yet." She squinted through the darkness. Her uncle's house was still a few blocks away.

"Listen to me, Scout." Max searched her face for a moment before allowing his gaze to meet hers. "I know you want to believe that voice was really your uncle's, but it couldn't have been. He's dead and you know it."

She exhaled heavily. "I realize that this could be a trick. Probably is. But I can't risk the possibility that it's not. I have to know."

To her surprise, he said, "I understand." He looked deeply into her eyes for a long while before continuing. "I just don't want you to be hurt, that's all. So let's do this my way. Let me go in first."

A tiny ripple of awareness went through her. He really did care about her… He wanted to protect her. And she definitely sensed that it was more than his assignment. She should tell him the truth now. Just blurt it out.

"You can trust me, Scout," he added when she would have spoken. "I won't ever break my word to you. It's my first rule in life—you're only as good as your word. You don't have anything if you don't have trust.''

A new kind of anxiety took root deep inside her. Not only had she failed to trust him, she'd lied to him. Lied by omission. Broken his trust by keeping this secret from him. If there'd been any doubt in her mind as to whether he would hold her decision against her, there wasn't now.

He would never forgive her.

He put the SUV into motion again and parked a block north of the house. She pushed away the hurt that wanted to take center stage in her thoughts. She had to focus right now. There would be time to grieve this newest loss later.

At least she hoped there would be.

If this was a trap…

Max moved along the hedge between Atkins's house and the closest neighbor. There was no vehicle in the driveway, but that didn't mean anything. Whoever had lured Scout here could have parked anywhere. During the four hours he'd insisted they wait before coming here, Max had asked Ryan Braxton to gather background intelligence on Biogenisis. The corporation was not as large as Alexon, but appeared extremely aggressive in their business tactics. They had been involved in two lawsuits and a federal investigation in the past three years. Each time, they'd skated out of trouble by the skin of their teeth. Biogenisis, in Max's opinion, was run by ruthless people who would go to any lengths to accomplish their goals.

Like getting their hands on Scout's baby.

Braxton had also passed on the results of the document analysis. The papers found at Harold Atkins's house were from a different manufacturer than the correspondence stock the Colby Agency had received from Alexon. Though that wasn't absolute proof in itself, it added to Max's growing certainty that Alexon was not the worst of the bad guys in this.

When he rounded the corner near the garage, a figure stepped out of the shadows.

Gage Kimble.

With his weapon cocked and leveled on target, Max hissed a curse and glared at the man. "What're you doing here?"

"I could ask you the same thing," Kimble plied just as smugly. His gun was drawn, too. He and Max stood three or four feet apart, weapons aimed at each other.

"Gage!" Scout lowered her own weapon and moved closer. Max had insisted she stay well behind him. Good thing she hadn't been too far behind him, she mused, because these two seemed ready to shoot each other on the spot just for the hell of it.

Gage glanced at her, then did a double take. "What happened to your arm?" Max took advantage of his distraction and made an aggressive maneuver, ultimately disarming Gage.

Scout rolled her eyes. Men. They just had to outdo each other. "Someone shot me," she said in answer to Gage's question. "What're you doing here?"

Belatedly, confusion assailed her. Why would Gage be hanging around her uncle's place? Max had said he'd shown up here before, told him that lie about the baby…. Things had been too chaotic for her to dwell on anything related to Gage ever since.

But now she wondered why he would say such a thing or how he'd even known about the baby.

"I've been watching your uncle's house for days hoping to catch you. We need to talk." He glanced at Max. "Privately."

Scout was just about to agree when Max intervened.

"No way." He shoved the confiscated weapon into the waistband of his jeans. "You can start talking all right. You can tell us what the hell you're really doing here."

Gage scowled at Max, then looked to Scout. "I got a call a few minutes ago. From Harold. He told me to come here right away. That it was urgent. He apparently didn't know I was already here. I've scarcely slept."

"In case you missed the funeral," Max said, leaving no room for doubt that he literally despised the man to whom he spoke, "Harold Atkins is dead."

"Be that as it may," Gage said, his own annoyance flaring, "I know Harold's voice. It was his voice."

Scout's heart was pounding now. It hadn't been her imagination, thank God. In the back of her mind she'd worried that maybe she was losing touch with reality. That'd she'd only imagined the voice. But Gage had heard it, too. Relief surged through her.

It still didn't make sense.

"I saw him murdered," she said, thinking aloud. She shook her head. "He couldn't have survived." At least she didn't think he could have. What if she was wrong?

"Can we go inside?" Gage urged, glancing

around anxiously. "I don't like being in the open like this."

"Got something to hide?" Max growled. "I'll just bet you do."

"Come on, Max," Scout implored, "let's go inside."

He insisted on checking out the place first. Gage was right on his heels every step of the way. Any minute now Scout expected them to start marking territory like her big old German shepherd back home. God, she missed that dog. But Donna would take good care of him until Scout got back there.

Scout studied the photographs on the mantel in the living room while the men did their thing. She smiled as the memories tumbled through her mind. Life had been so simple when she'd been a little girl. She hadn't had a mother, but she'd had a father and an adopted uncle who'd both loved her dearly. Harold had been in the military with her dad, but an injury had forced him into early retirement. Lucky for Scout. He'd played nanny anytime her father had to be away on a mission where she wasn't allowed to go.

Pain flashed through her. It would really be nice if he was still alive, but she simply didn't see how that was possible.

"We should get out of here," Gage suggested, sounding nervous as he and Max returned to the living room.

"Enough, Kimble. First we have to come inside, now we have to leave. I want to know the real reason you're here." Max's fury had not abated, but he looked every bit as worried as Gage appeared to be.

"If Harold's not here and we were both lured to

this house…'' Gage allowed the statement to fade into unspoken innuendo.

Scout swore. ''You're right.''

Max was already hauling her out of the house when the realization of danger made her spring into action. As soon as they cleared the door, they all ran like hell.

As their footsteps slapped against the asphalt street a whoosh sounded behind them and then a blaze of light lit up half the block. The house burst into flames as if the whole thing had been doused with an accelerant.

Braxton and Doug joined them near Max's SUV. ''What happened?''

''It was a setup,'' Max answered, his accusing gaze going directly to Gage.

Scout shook her head. ''But that's crazy. Why would they kill me?'' Her hand went automatically to her tummy. If they'd killed her they would have killed the baby. Without the baby, what was the point of all this?

''Can we talk now?'' Gage demanded. He looked straight at her, pointedly ignoring Max's murderous glower.

She nodded. ''I guess we should.''

MAX COULDN'T KEEP HER from talking to Kimble, but he damn sure had the final say about what the ground rules would be. They'd left the scene just as the fire department arrived and only seconds before the police had shown up. Victoria would have more smoothing over to do. Chicago PD as well as FD didn't like witnesses leaving the scene before they were questioned.

Kimble was accompanied to the Colby Agency by Braxton and Cooper. Max and Scout drove over together. She wanted to complain about his domineering tactics, but she'd thought better of it when she took a closer look at him as they climbed into his SUV. He was pretty sure his expression wasn't pleasant, but he didn't care. He didn't want Kimble even looking at her, much less talking to her.

But his more rational side, the one he'd beaten down for the moment, knew that they had to hear him out just in case he had relevant information.

When this was over, Max intended to kick the guy's ass.

Cooper had prepared a pot of coffee. Braxton took a seat at the long conference table while Max and Kimble blatantly sized each other up.

"Whether you want to believe it or not, your uncle is involved in the threat to you," Kimble said, turning his attention to Scout.

"What makes you think someone is threatening me?"

Good girl, Max cheered silently. *Give him hell.* Something was way off with this guy. Simon was running a check on him. They would soon know.

She folded her arms over her middle and leaned against the conference table. "I didn't tell you I was being threatened."

Kimble didn't look the least bit put off. "Donna told me. I called to check on you a few weeks ago and she told me you were missing in action. Then last week she called and told me *everything.*"

Scout narrowed her eyes suspiciously. "She wasn't supposed to tell anyone."

Kimble sighed. "I admit it—I had to coerce the

information out of her.'' He moved closer to Scout. Max tensed. ''But she knows how I feel about you.'' He reached out and touched her shoulder then. A red mist swam before Max's eyes. It was all he could do to hold himself back.

''She knows what we've shared,'' Kimble said intimately.

Scout drew away from his touch. ''Then she must also know that you left me in the lurch!''

Max wanted to crush him. Kimble had hurt her. He'd gotten her pregnant and then walked away. Death would be too good for the bastard.

Kimble nodded. ''Guilty,'' he agreed woefully. ''But I had my reasons.''

Scout looked as skeptical as Max felt. ''Oh really?'' she retorted. ''And what were those?''

Kimble shoved his hands into his pockets, and all three Colby agents in the room reacted at once. Though he'd been patted down, there were always new ways to hide a weapon.

He pulled his hands free of his pockets and showed that they were empty. ''Satisfied?'' He looked from one man to the other before turning his attention back to Scout. ''You won't want to accept this news, but it's the truth and it's time you knew.''

Max put aside his raging emotions and focused on the man speaking. He refused to consider why the two of them steered clear of the ''baby'' subject. He was sure Kimble had been referring to the baby when he'd said the assistant had told him ''everything.''

''Harold Atkins killed your father.''

''What?'' Scout's expression turned to one of utter disbelief. "That's insane. Harold and my father were like brothers."

"At one time." Kimble shook his head. "After Harold's retirement from the military he got mixed up with some bad sorts. He started selling military secrets to settle the score. He got away with it for a long time, even while he and your father worked together as P.I.'s. It wasn't until after he'd gone to work at Alexon that your father discovered the truth. Your father confronted him. Threatened to turn him in. Harold killed him to prevent that from happening."

Scout shook her head in denial. "I don't believe you."

"It's true. Your father told me of his concerns. By the time I could get back to him with the information he needed to seal Harold's fate, he was dead." Gage exhaled loudly. "There was nothing I could do. It was too late."

Scout pushed off from the table and rounded on him. "If Harold really killed my father, why didn't you turn him in? You knew how badly I wanted to find my dad's killer." She spoke the words calmly enough, but the obvious fury building beneath had Max moving closer in case she physically attacked Kimble.

"Because," the man explained, "he told me he'd kill you if I ever said a word, if I ever came near you again. I couldn't take that risk."

Silence screamed in the room for three excruciating beats.

"But you did come back," she countered, her voice trembling now.

Max wanted desperately to go to her, but he knew Scout too well. She wouldn't want to look weak.

"Yes. I wanted to make sure you were all right. Harold was in Chicago. I'd hoped he wouldn't find out…but he did. I couldn't risk him hurting you. So I dropped out of sight again."

If Max had to endure one more second of this guy's BS, he'd puke. With the way his gut still roiled, that possibility wasn't far off base.

"So you've told me," Scout said tightly. "What now?"

He shrugged. "Considering the phone call we both got, I'm concerned that Harold faked his death. He's in this with Alexon, I'm sure of it. You have to be very careful, Scout."

"If he's alive and in cahoots with Alexon, why would he try to kill me?"

She wasn't buying it. Max was immensely proud of her. The whole incident at the house was completely off. Somehow. What good would she and the baby be to anyone dead? He shuddered at the idea.

"I think that little stunt was meant for me. He knew these guys—" Kimble hitched a thumb toward Max "—would take care of you."

What a neat little package Scout's ex had tied everything into. Too bad Max didn't believe him for a second.

"Time's up, Kimble." Max moved between him and Scout. "We're calling it a night. Do I have to tell you that we don't want to hear from you again?"

Kimble looked from Max to Scout, who said nothing. Pride welled in Max that she had, with her silence, backed him up.

"Come on, Kimble," Cooper said. "I'll give you a ride back to your car."

When Cooper and Kimble had exited the conference room, Max focused his full attention on Scout. "You know he's lying through his teeth, don't you?"

She looked tired and uncertain. Dammit. He hated for her to suffer any more traumas. Damn Kimble.

"I wish I could be sure." She shook her head in weary defeat. "His accusations would explain some things I've never understood."

Max didn't want to consider that she was probably rationalizing Kimble's disappearance with this crap. Would that make her want to reconcile with him? Max clenched his jaw. He refused to believe she could be that blind.

"Miss Jackson." Ryan Braxton stood and moved toward her.

Scout had almost forgotten about him, he'd been so quiet. She offered him a pathetic excuse for a smile. He was quieter than the other Colby agents she'd met. But she was certain that still waters ran particularly deep in his case. There was a weariness in his eyes that spoke to her. Somehow he'd been here before...far too many times. "Yes?"

"Whoever delivered that cellphone to you is managing to keep up with your movements particularly well, and in spite of all our precautions. I'm wondering if perhaps you may unknowingly be carrying a tracking device."

The thought hadn't occurred to her. She supposed it wasn't impossible. "I don't know." The frown she wore deepened. "Anything's possible, I guess."

There were other questions she'd wanted to ask Gage...but couldn't. Not in front of Max.

"Why don't we leave your personal belongings at the guest house before relocating you this time?" Ryan suggested.

She shrugged. "Okay."

"I'll call Amy Wells and have her pick up a few things and bring them over." Ryan's gaze traveled the length of her. "Size 6?"

Amazed at his accuracy, she nodded mutely.

"You'll need to leave your jewelry, as well." He looked directly at her locket.

"I never take it off," she protested. "My father gave it to me." She'd taken it off only that once, when she'd been in isolation with Max at Alexon.

"For just a little while. Once we've had it checked thoroughly I'll see that it's returned to you immediately."

Reluctantly, she nodded. What else could she do? Someone was dogging her every step. This time she'd barely escaped a deadly fire bomb. She couldn't take any more chances.

Not when her baby was counting on her.

TWO HOURS HAD PASSED before they'd left the agency. Max had driven around another hour to make sure he had no tail. Scout had fallen asleep in the passenger seat. She was exhausted, physically and mentally. He wished he could shield her fully from the rest of this, but that might prove impossible. But he would do everything in his power to keep her safe and to help her outsmart the Biogenisis people or whoever the hell was after her. Simon's check on Kimble had given them nothing. After leaving the military the man had ceased to exist. There was nothing on him. Whatever he was up to, it would not be in Scout's best interests. Simon wanted to look further, to see if he could tie him to Biogenisis.

Simon had kindly offered his penthouse. With the warning, of course, that Max take better care of it than he had his SUV. For the first time since that night at the cemetery, Max thought of his own home. What kind of damage had been done there? He pushed away the scenarios that came immediately to mind. Right now he was too tired to care.

After parking in the underground garage of the prestigious building Simon called home, Max gently shook Scout's shoulder.

She roused instantly. Her father had trained her well. The daughter of a colonel wouldn't be lax even when she slept.

"I'm up." She immediately surveyed her surroundings and climbed out of the vehicle.

Max did the same.

In the elevator, he inserted Simon's key and they were carried directly to the fourteenth floor. The door opened onto an elegant foyer that led straight into Simon's penthouse apartment.

"Wow, your friend must be loaded," Scout commented as they moved into the main living area. The view from the wall of windows was nothing short of spectacular.

"He's like Cooper," Max said without malice, "born to it." It didn't really bother Max at all that his friends were better off financially than he was. He wouldn't trade his close-knit family for all the money in the world. Neither Cooper nor Simon had those kinds of ties. Well, Simon was working on making a family with his new wife Jolie.

"I think I'll just lie down."

"How about I drum up some dinner?" Max offered. "I'm sure Simon's got anything your heart would desire." He added a smile, hoping to encourage her. He felt fairly certain he could manage to eat now.

She did smile back, just a little. "I'm not very hungry. Thanks, anyway."

Kimble, the son of a bitch, had really done a number on her emotions. Max wanted to strangle the jerk.

Before she could get away, he said, "I meant what I said. I won't let anyone hurt you. Not even Kimble."

She turned back, her eyes suspiciously bright, but intensely determined. "You know what I have to do, don't you?"

The hair on the back of Max's neck prickled. He didn't like this. She sounded resigned to some cruel fate.

"The only way we'll ever know who the real bad guys are is if we lure them into a trap."

"No." He was already shaking his head before she completed the statement.

As if he hadn't said it, she went on. "To set a trap you need bait. It's the only way."

He strode across the room and took her by the arms, careful to avoid her wound. "I won't let you do that. It's too risky."

She laughed, but there was no humor in the sound. "Don't worry, Max. Despite what happened at my uncle's house, they won't hurt me. They have to keep me alive until the baby is born.''

He glanced at the bandage on her arm. ''We can't be sure, and I'm not taking any chances with you or your baby. I don't care who the father is. I can't let you take that risk.''

''I'll never be safe unless we draw them out and bring them down,'' she said softly, her voice quaking again. ''Never. And you know it.''

God, she was right. He didn't want to admit it, but she was. How could they stop an enemy whose identity they didn't know? They couldn't. It was that simple and, at the same time, that complex.

If they didn't make a move, the enemy would. It was only a matter of time before they caught them in a vulnerable position.

Using her and her unborn child as bait was the only way to draw them out on Max's terms.

He pulled her close to him. He wanted to hold her...to kiss her, but he held back, not wanting to cross that line, yet needing to so very much. ''You remember what I said, Scout. All that matters is that you and the baby are safe. I don't care about anything else.''

He didn't have to worry about crossing the line.

She took the initiative.

She kissed him.

Chapter Thirteen

Scout drew back and stared into his eyes. In that moment she wondered whether, if her baby was a boy, he would look like his father. Would he have that thick, sandy-colored hair and those sky-blue eyes that could make her shiver with just a glance? A little blond-haired, blue-eyed girl would be equally wonderful.

A twinge of fear abruptly replaced her foolish musings. Would this man ever forgive her for lying to him? For keeping the truth from him even at a moment like this? She'd wanted desperately to demand that Gage explain why he'd told Max he was the baby's father, or even how he knew about her pregnancy. But she hadn't been able to bring herself to allow Max to learn the truth that way. And the truth would certainly have come out in the course of the conversation. If Scout had her guess, Donna had probably spilled the beans to Gage about that along with the rest. He had said she'd told him *everything*. Still, he had to know the baby wasn't his. Maybe he hoped to reconcile with her and had told Max that lie to make him back off. But she didn't want to think about that right now.

She moistened her lips, and Max's hungry gaze followed the movement. She could tell him now.... She could. There was no doubt in her mind that she could trust Max completely. That he cared deeply. But she had to know more. If there was any possibility they might have a future together she had to be certain it was about more than just the baby.

Maybe she was being selfish...but she still had to know.

"Scout, we should—"

"Shh." She pressed her fingers to his lips. "Don't say anything. Don't even think." She lifted her mouth to his once more and whispered, "Just feel."

He kissed her more deeply this time. She could feel him letting go, putting the rules and all the other stuff out of his mind. She wanted this moment to eclipse all else. It belonged to them....

He lifted her in his arms and carried her to the bedroom, stopping in the middle of the room and settling her onto her feet. As in the room they'd just left, the view was magnificent. An unveiled wall of windows overlooked the city with its twinkling lights and soaring skyscrapers.

The bedroom was lavish. A wide, inviting king-size bed served as a regal focal point. Thick carpeting and handsome wood furnishings completed the picture. She sighed.

Max was watching her, she suddenly realized. He stood perfectly still, those analyzing eyes taking in her captivation with the lovely surroundings. She knew what he must be thinking. She turned to him and moved in close. Her arms went up and around his neck, and her breasts tingled as she leaned against his chest. His arms went instantly around her.

"This is a great apartment," she said, then nipped his lower lip with her teeth. His breath caught. "But I like your place a lot better."

He swallowed tightly. She watched the movement with utter fascination. This would be their first time together *alone*.

"No one's watching, you know," she murmured. Her heart thundered savagely. She wanted him to make love to her. The yearning was so fierce she could scarcely draw a breath. But still he hesitated. He wanted to kiss her; she knew he did. She could feel the tension in his strong body...could feel the hardness of his own desire pressing against her belly. All she had to do was crank up the persuasion.

Max was certain he had never wanted anything as much as he wanted the woman in his arms. But was she thinking clearly? Or was it the overwhelming stress, the betrayal she still felt where Kimble was concerned? Every muscle in his body jerked at the thought of Kimble. He despised the bastard.

"What about Kimble?" he managed to say tightly.

She sighed, those gray eyes glittering with desire. Just the way he remembered from their time together four months ago. She'd looked at him this way then, as well...only there was more this time. Something indefinable. Did she want to make love with him just to have revenge against her lover?

Max closed his eyes and forced the probable answer from his mind. He couldn't bear the thought. Couldn't bear the idea of her being with *him*.

"I don't know what Gage has to do with any of

this," she said firmly, her words forcing his eyes open so he could read hers as she spoke. "I haven't seen him in months. Wouldn't care if I never saw him again. Whatever I once felt for him is long gone."

Max wanted to believe her, saw the truth of her statement in her eyes. But when the child was born, would she still feel the same way? When Kimble demanded his rights as a father, what would she do then? Would her relationship with Max be strong enough to withstand her need to keep her child safe and happy?

"You may feel differently when—"

She cut off his words, rising on tiptoe and closing her mouth over his. "No more talk," she murmured between kisses.

He let it go then; he couldn't help himself. He wanted her too much. Needed her too desperately. He surrendered completely to the kiss, relishing the sweet taste of her and the excitement he could feel thrumming through her slender body. She wanted him and nothing else mattered.

Undressing her slowly, he rained kisses over her newly bared shoulders, across the lush swells of her breasts. Her fingers dived into his hair and she held him more firmly against her, silently urging him on. She toed off her sneakers as he dropped to his knees before her. He lowered the zipper of her jeans and unhurriedly eased them down. She braced her hands on his shoulders as she stepped out of the confining fabric. While peeling off her socks, he measured each small foot in his hands. She was so beautifully made, all the way down to her sexy little toes.

Once she was naked save for the bra and panties,

he looked up at her, telling her with his eyes how beautiful she was and how much he wanted her. He flattened a palm on her abdomen and smoothed it across the creamy soft flesh there. He would care for this child just as he cared for her...if she allowed him to. He pressed a kiss beneath her belly button and she quivered. He kissed her there again and she gasped.

He laved her skin with his tongue, needing to taste all of her, and praying that he would have the strength and discipline to take his time. She reached behind her and released her bra, then shrugged it off. His pulse leaped at the sight of her unrestrained breasts. He kissed each one, nuzzled his face there and inhaled her feminine scent.

She urged him to his feet and gave him the same treatment—undressing him slowly, touching and tasting each newly bared part of him until he cried out savagely. She kissed her way along the length of him, ignoring his labored breathing and his tortured groans.

Finally, he could take no more and swept her off her feet and onto the bed. He kissed her, tasting the saltiness of his own flesh on her sweet lips. She returned his kiss with abandon. Their bodies were on fire, writhing and undulating, needing, searching for contact.

He pushed between her thighs, going in slowly despite the urgency pounding through him with every panting breath. She made a desperate sound and wiggled her hips, arching upward. He tried to hold back, to take it slow, as he'd promised himself he would, but she was making that promise impossible.

"Wait," he pleaded. He didn't want to risk hurting her. It was all he could do to hold back. His body pulsed with the need to drive into her until—

She kissed him hard, derailing his thought. "I don't want to wait!" she breathed, kissing him again and again until he groaned savagely.

She was relentless, surging upward to meet him, faster, harder until he couldn't catch his breath. He could feel her muscles tightening around him, gripping him like a hot vise. She suddenly stilled and cried out, propelling him over the edge with her. Control evaporated. He drove himself to release, bursting with it while she still clenched rhythmically around him.

Long minutes later they lay side by side, their arms and legs entangled, both still breathing hard from the frantic coming together.

"I don't want to lose you again, Scout," he said, his courage bolstered by their mating. He needed her to know how he felt. He turned to look into her eyes. "I can't let you do this. It's too risky for you…and the baby."

Scout blinked furiously to hold back her tears. He didn't want her to take any more risks. More important, he cared enough about her to accept this baby even though he didn't know it was his child. "Max." It was past time to tell him the truth. Whatever the consequences, she couldn't keep this secret a moment longer.

He traced a path along the line of her jaw with one fingertip. "Just tell me that you'll do as I say, and I'll be happy." He grinned, knowing full well that she wasn't about to be bossed around by anyone. His expression turned somber then. "I'm serious, Scout. I don't want you to be hurt. We'll find another way.''

''But—''

He shook his head. ''No buts. It's too risky. I don't want you in the line of fire.'' He pressed a kiss next to the dressing on her arm. ''This—'' he gestured to the bandage ''—could have been a lot worse. If you won't do it for your own safety, think about the baby.''

A cold, hard realization dawned on her then. If she told him the truth, he'd have her under lock and key so fast it would make her head swim. If he had the slightest suspicion that this was his child, she'd be out of here before she could blink an eye. Max just didn't get it. She and the baby would never be safe if the enemy wasn't nailed. She would be on the run and looking over her shoulder forever—or at least until someone came up with the antidote for K-141. Either scenario was too long. She sighed, reveling in the feel of his muscular body resting along the length of hers. She hated to do this, but she was going to have to keep her secret a little longer. Or maybe she was just a coward and would use any rationalization not to tell him. That, she admitted, was more likely the truth of the matter.

''I'm sorry, Max,'' she said finally. ''I have to do this. And I need you to help me.''

Exhaling in exasperation, he rested his forehead against hers. ''Do I have a choice?''

''Nope.''

He kissed her, just the briefest meeting of lips, but she felt the tenderness and sweetness all the way to her heart. ''All right. We'll do this your way.''

He looked deeply into her eyes. "But when this is over, we do things my way."

"Deal."

Scout knew then and there that she could spend the rest of her life right here in his arms without ever looking back.

She prayed she would get the chance.

"YOU'RE SURE THE LOCKET was never out of your sight?"

Scout was damn tired of answering the same question over and over. She glowered at Max. "I told you it was never out of my sight other than when Alexon kept it while we were in isolation."

"No other time?" Max pressed.

"No…other…time," she said succinctly. She never took off the locket. Her father had given it to her when she was sixteen. She'd worn it ever since. The three weeks they'd been in isolation at Alexon was the only time it hadn't been on her person.

Max paced over to the wall of windows and stared out at the inspiring view offered by Simon's elegant home.

"But," Ryan Braxton countered from his relaxed position on the arm of the sofa, "you do sleep. The bug could have been planted while you were sleeping."

She shrugged, tired of this game of twenty questions. She wanted to do something. Sitting here was driving her crazy. She'd felt so guilty about not telling Max the truth about the baby that she'd been irritable all day. It was almost two o'clock now. She wanted to act!

"Sure," she admitted. "I suppose someone could

have done it while I slept.'' Her uncle Harold had spent the night at her place in Houston a couple of times, just as she'd stayed over with him a time or two. But he was dead, wasn't he? Just to be certain, Cooper was checking with the medical examiner as well as the mortician to see if photos of the body were available. Her stomach roiled. She wasn't sure she was up to looking at pictures of her uncle's dead body, or anyone else's, for that matter. Besides, why would he hurt her? He'd loved her…hadn't he?

''Someone planted the tracking device in your locket, and that's how they've known where you were no matter what precautions we took to spirit you away.'' Max braced his hands at his waist and turned to face her. ''As much as it goes against my initial hunch, all evidence points toward Alexon.''

Ryan nodded in agreement. ''Motive, opportunity, means—it's all there.''

Max shook his head. ''But it just doesn't feel right. Maybe it was your old friend Kimble.'' He tossed out the suggestion, his tone icy.

''Gage has nothing to do with any of this. You just don't want to believe it's Alexon,'' Scout argued, taking umbrage at his innuendo. ''I know it's them. I was there, being held hostage. I know what I went through.''

She was right. Max couldn't argue with that. He was pretty sure Alexon—Brandon—was hiding something. But to assume the company had orchestrated all this just didn't *feel* right. He preferred to focus on Kimble. Mainly because he hated the guy.

''Here.'' He offered the necklace back to Scout. ''We've taken care of the bug.'' They'd also taken another step that she didn't need to know about. She took the delicate chain and locket from him and immediately placed it around her slender neck. Max looked away. He wanted her again...desperately. With extreme difficulty he forced his attention back to the matter at hand.

The beep of the security system warned that someone was coming up via the elevator that opened directly into Simon's apartment. Cooper, most likely since Simon's wife Jolie was in Atlanta visiting her father. Still, tension radiated through Max. He didn't like where this was heading. Scout was determined to go through with the whole baiting scheme, but another plan was already underway. She might not go along with it, but he would try his best to convince her.

The elevator doors slid open and Cooper stepped into the foyer. He shook his head at their expectant gazes. "The mortician didn't take any photographs, although he did look at the photograph I showed him of Harold Atkins and said that it could have been the body he prepped for burial."

"Could have been?" Scout stepped forward. "He didn't make a positive ID?"

Cooper shook his head again. "He said it wasn't possible, considering the gunshot exit wounds to the face. Besides, officials from Alexon ID'd him."

"Harold was shot once in the chest." Scout was the one shaking her head now. "That can't be right."

"But you had to make a run for it, correct?" Max said, instinctively moving closer to her. He couldn't bear the hurt she was being forced to relive. "The same shooter or even one of the other men could have fired more shots after you were out of there."

She scrubbed her hands over her face. "I suppose. I don't know. A shot was fired, Uncle Harold went down…I ran." She shrugged, the slump of her shoulders giving away the guilt she still felt at surviving when her uncle hadn't. But she'd been protecting the baby. "I don't know what happened after that."

"According to the mortician there were two shots to the back of the head. But you haven't heard the strangest part," Cooper said, drawing their attention back to him. "The M.E.'s file on Harold Atkins is missing."

The tension in the room rose to a new level.

Max and Braxton exchanged a look. "That news certainly adds a fresh twist," Braxton commented offhandedly. "Either Harold Atkins is still alive or—"

"Someone wants us to think he is," Max finished for him.

"Why would someone want us to think he's alive?" Scout demanded, emotion making her slow to comprehend the possibilities.

She looked confused and tired, and Max wanted to hold her and assure her that it would be all right. But at the moment he had to keep his distance. It was the only way he'd ever be able to deny her what she wanted when the time came.

And even then it wasn't going to be easy.

"What about Kimble?" It was Braxton who raised the subject this time. "How does he play into all this?"

Max tensed. Even the sound of the guy's name made him want to break something, specifically the jerk's neck. "I think he may be involved," he allowed, knowing full well that the statement was partly motivated by his hatred for him.

"I don't see how," Scout countered. "We dated for a while once but that was months ago. We broke up and that was it."

Max's gaze connected with hers and she looked away. He wanted to ask about the baby. He wanted to grill her until his ego was assuaged where the other man was concerned. Instead he forced himself to calm down. Losing it on the subject of Kimble wasn't going to help.

"How did the two of you become acquainted?" Braxton prodded. He stood and stretched and headed to the bar that separated the living room from the kitchen.

"He was a new SF recruit under my father's tutelage," she explained as she stepped forward and accepted the bottle of water he offered.

"By SF you mean special forces?" Braxton twisted off the top of his own bottle and took a long swallow.

She nodded and did the same.

Max kept his mouth shut. He was too close to this and he knew it. Braxton knew it, too. That's why he had taken the lead. Max didn't mind Braxton's move; it was the right thing to do. Though Ryan Braxton preferred working the research and evidential side of cases, his presence now was definitely welcome. What Max did mind was his own inability to separate his personal feelings from the job.

And why wouldn't he have trouble?

He was in love with the woman.

Everything inside him stilled as the knowledge echoed through him. It was true. He'd been in love with her from the beginning. Four months of separation and a pregnancy hadn't changed anything.

"My father brought him home a few times when he was on leave." She shrugged. "I never saw him again until almost a year after my father died. Gage was devastated by the news. He stayed around the Texas area for a while and we...dated. Things got a little serious for a while."

Max clenched his jaw and forced himself to look anywhere but at her. He didn't want to hear this part, but he had no choice. They had to determine Kimble's involvement, if any. His showing up twice now was pushing the probability of coincidence.

"And then he disappeared again," Braxton suggested.

She sipped her water and said, "Yeah. I didn't see him again until a couple weeks after Max and I were released from isolation at Alexon."

And they'd had dinner, Max added silently. *Dinner and sex.* His heart drummed against his sternum as his mind conjured the images that accompanied the thought. Hurt stabbed deep into his heart and very nearly paralyzed it. *That was the past,* he told himself again. He would not hold the past against her or the baby she carried.

He forced himself to look at Scout...to see nothing but the woman he loved. The other images and thoughts evaporated like water on a sun-scorched rock. Now was all that mattered.

"Did he, to your knowledge, have any dealings with your uncle?"

Scout shook her head. "They'd met once while we were dating, but didn't act as if they knew each other. My uncle never mentioned him and vice versa.''

Braxton considered the information for a time, as did Max. ''His lack of recent commitment or involvement in your life makes him an unlikely participant,'' Max said, taking the lead again now that his emotions were back under control. ''But his sudden appearance in the middle of all this prevents me from being able to completely rule him out as a suspect.''

Scout splayed one hand, palm up. ''I can see that. His abrupt appearance is suspicious to me as well. But he's strange like that.'' She frowned. ''I noticed it when my father first introduced him to me. You never could tell exactly what Gage was thinking. He's too good at hiding his feelings.'' She chewed her lower lip a moment. Max remembered vividly the taste of that succulent lip. She went on, drawing his attention back to the discussion. ''Maybe it was part of the covert training he received in the military or something. He's impossible to read.''

Max, too, had noted Kimble's ability to keep his expression unreadable. He was quite good at acting. But Max had worried that his dislike for the man had affected his reasoning.

''So, we move to the next phase of the strategy,'' Braxton offered.

Scout's head came up at that. ''We have a plan?'' She looked from Braxton to Max. ''No one mentioned a plan to me.''

This was going to be the hard part. ''I talked to Cooper while you were sleeping,'' Max admitted, knowing she would be as mad as hell.

Sure enough, a look of fury stole across her face. "And you didn't bother mentioning it to me."

"When Cooper called and explained your dilemma," Braxton interrupted when Max would have spoken, "Simon Ruhl made the final decision."

Startled, Max gazed at Braxton. He was taking the heat off him, allowing Scout to consider Simon himself the culprit. Simon had, in fact, made the decision. Manuevers this dicey weren't made without approval from the next level. But Max had been willing to suffer the repercussions. Relief speared through him now. He would owe his colleague a huge debt of gratitude if they pulled this off. Knowing how stubborn Scout could be, Max had seriously worried that he wouldn't be able to talk her into seeing things his way. Now he didn't have to.

"Max will call Alexon and set up a meeting to negotiate the conditions of your cooperation—"

"Who said I'm cooperating with them?" Scout snapped. She shot Max a look. "Was that your idea?"

"The goal," Max explained, "is to make them think we're willing to negotiate, to draw them out. If they're planning to make a move against you, they'll do it then. We need to know if Alexon really is the enemy."

Scout relaxed marginally. Okay, she could see that. She wanted to draw out the enemy himself. She'd just expected to be in on the planning stage as well as the execution. That she'd been left out stung her ego. After what she and Max had shared last night, she'd expected him to be open and honest with her. She stopped herself midthought. How could she expect that from him, when she hadn't been completely honest in turn?

"If Alexon is on the up and up, the meeting will go without a hitch," Ryan commented. "If, however, they aren't, we'll know by their actions."

"So, what time are we meeting them?"

Max and Ryan exchanged another of those looks, then Ryan said, "It would be in your best interest to stay clear of the heat." When she would have told him what she thought, he quelled her tirade with a look that made her want to take a step back. "If you truly want to protect your child, you'll stay out of harm's way. Think about where your priorities lie, Miss Jackson." He said the last with a pointed glance at her bandaged arm.

All the fight drained out of her then. They were right. She couldn't take any more chances with her baby's life. She'd been a fool to think she could bring down Alexon on her own or even with help. That would only put her health and that of her child at risk.

She nodded reluctantly. "Agreed."

The next hour was a whirlwind of activity. Unbeknownst to her, the meeting with Alexon had already been arranged. Nicole Reed Michaels would again pose as Scout and accompany Max. Ryan Braxton would provide backup. Cooper would keep Scout company in the penthouse, where she would be safe. She and Max had discussed the extent of her cooperation, present and future, with Alexon, if any.

Still, she wanted to scream in frustration. She wanted to be out there, forcing Alexon to admit the truth, and watching Max's back. But she couldn't. She had to think of the baby.

Fear gripped her. She couldn't let Max do this without knowing the truth. If something happened to him...

Her heart in her throat, she crossed the room and tugged him away from the group. "We need to talk."

He glanced at the others, then allowed her to lead him to the bedroom. The sheets were still tousled and the scent of their lovemaking still lingered in the air. Her eyes burned with the sudden, almost overwhelming need to cry.

"Don't worry." He kissed her cheek, his strong arms suddenly around her waist. "Everything's going to be fine. Trust me."

She smiled, struggling to keep the tears at bay for just another moment. "I do trust you, Max." His smile tipped the scales, making her lose the battle. Hot tears streamed down her cheeks. His heartrending expression faded into a frown. "I haven't been totally up front with you," she said, her voice shaky.

"Scout, don't cry." He brushed the tears from her cheeks. "Whatever it is, it won't change how I feel." His smile returned full force. "I love you, you know."

The bottom dropped out of her stomach, but she had to tell him before she lost her nerve. "This baby is yours, Max. I don't know why you hadn't considered the possibility or why you believed anything Gage said. But it's yours. That's why Alexon kept tabs on me even after they released me. They knew I'd conceived while in isolation with you, and that's what started all this."

"But—"

She shook her head. "No buts." She repeated the words he'd said to her last night. "It's true. This is your child."

Chapter Fourteen

Max leaned against his SUV at the designated meeting place and tried to slow the thoughts whirling inside his head. He had to stay focused here. The Alexon officials would arrive at any moment and he had to be ready. Braxton was in position on a nearby rooftop. If there was trouble he would step in. Nicole waited in the SUV, the black wig disguising her blond hair. Ian Michaels, her husband and Victoria's second in command, had insisted on providing additional backup, and was somewhere close by.

Not that Max could blame him. He wouldn't want his wife in a dangerous situation without him around, either.

Wife.

Child.

The words tumbled one over the other in his head. Though he didn't have a wife—yet, he amended—he did have a child on the way. The realization shook him to the core of his being. He wanted to be angry that Scout had kept the truth from him, but somehow he couldn't. He was far too awestruck by the whole concept.

The child she carried was his.

Fury flared inside him. Kimble had known that; that's why he'd lied to Max in the first place. If Kimble wasn't the father and still knew about the pregnancy, that put him back at the top of the suspect list. Max knew what he'd tried to do. Kimble had wanted to throw him off balance, to drive a wedge between him and Scout. Well, it hadn't worked. Max cared enough for Scout that the child's paternity hadn't mattered to him. One way or another Max would get to the bottom of Gage Kimble's involvement.

But now it definitely did. The child was his and he damn well intended to be a part of its life. It was no longer a matter of whether or not he and Scout could work something out, they *would* work something out. He loved her. He wanted her. And he would stop this threat to her one way or another. He'd have done that either way, but now he had an even stronger motivation to get it done quickly. His child would not come into this world with a threat looming over its head.

"Show time," Max muttered under his breath when a pair of headlights came into view. They all wore communicators—state-of-the-art earpieces that were almost invisible to the naked eye, and tiny transmitter disks strategically placed on a lapel or collar.

"Copy that." Braxton's voice echoed in his earpiece.

"Relax," Nicole murmured next. "Your tension is showing, Max."

He glanced toward the SUV and forced a smile for the lady inside. He wondered if she knew she'd just asked the impossible of him.

A long, dark limousine rolled into the deserted lot outside the dilapidated warehouse Max had chosen as the rendezvous point. This would be done on his terms and his terms only.

A rear door opened and Regis Brandon emerged. He adjusted his designer suit jacket and strolled over to where Max waited. "Where's Miss Jackson?" he demanded, immediately suspicious.

Max inclined his head toward the passenger seat of his SUV. Brandon's gaze darted in that direction. With the dark tint he could only see that someone was in there, but couldn't make out the details.

"This is how it's going to be." Max straightened from the relaxed stance he'd forced his body into and looked the shorter man in the eye. "We do this my way or we don't do it at all."

"He's got six on the ground," Braxton warned, his voice a low murmur in Max's earpiece.

Max glanced past Brandon and saw a flicker of movement a few yards away.

"What's it going to take to get Miss Jackson's cooperation?" Brandon demanded, oblivious to Max's increased vigilance.

Dividing his attention between Brandon and the shifting shadows, Max spelled it out for him. "If Alexon is willing to provide documentation that their efforts are indeed commissioned by the United States government, Miss Jackson will turn over the umbilical cord at the time of birth." Max looked directly at him then. "But there will be no—absolutely no—further contact with her until that time. The birth will take place in the hospital of her choosing and with only one member of Alexon standing by. If Alexon ever attempts to contact Miss Jackson

or her child again, formal charges will be filed.''
Max gave him a long level look that relayed just
how serious he was. ''We have our contacts in the
government, as well. If Alexon ever wants to be
awarded another research contract, I would suggest
that you abide by the conditions.''

His features tight with fury, Brandon snapped his
fingers, and six men closed in on their position. All
six wore dark clothing and black ski masks—just as
Scout had described her attackers and the man who
had supposedly killed her uncle.

Max frowned. Could she have been right all
along? Surely he hadn't been this far off the mark.

''Standing ready,'' Braxton informed him, the
words reassuring in Max's ear.

''Falling down on your word already?'' Max demanded curtly.

Brandon shook his head. ''You don't understand,
Mr. Maxwell. Biogenisis will abide by no such conditions. If we don't take Miss Jackson into custody
and keep her safe until the child is born, Biogenisis
will. They'll snatch her right from under your nose
when you least expect it, and they won't care if she
or the child survives once they have what they
want.''

Max gestured to the men in ski masks, whose
weapons were aimed at him. ''And you do care
about her safety,'' he said tightly. ''That's why six
men have weapons trained on our position this very
moment. That's why your men shot at us the other
night and killed Harold Atkins one week ago. Is
Gage Kimble working for you, as well?''

Brandon held up a hand and the weapons lowered

instantly, surprising Max all over again. "What men? Who shot at you?"

"Why do you suppose we've been on the run?" Max flung the words at him. "Your men tracked us down at my cabin that very first night I found Scout. We could have been killed in the high-speed chase that ensued, not to mention in the firefight. And you're talking safety? Miss Jackson was hit. How are we supposed to trust you?"

Brandon's eyes bulged in horror. He couldn't have faked that look if he'd tried. "Is she all right? Dear God, no one told me about this!"

Another surprising response. "She's fine. It was only a flesh wound. Then last night her uncle's house burned to the ground and we were almost caught in the explosion. Your man Kimble was there," Max added, in hopes of slipping him up.

Brandon shook his head. "We had nothing to do with any of this. I've had no idea where you were. Of course I heard about the house in the news, but I didn't know she was there. And I certainly don't know anyone named Kimble. I haven't left my office in days for fear I'd miss a call from you." His breath caught. "Biogenisis. They're on to you somehow."

Max shrugged noncommittally. If Kimble wasn't working for Alexon, he had to be working for Biogenisis. Max's impression was no longer simply hinging on emotion. "Someone is. They had a tracking device implanted in her locket. But lucky for us, we discovered it in time."

Brandon shook his head. "You must believe me. They'll stop at nothing, use any means to get at her. If they perfect the antidote first, the U.S. will be at their mercy.'' He waved his arms, indicating his guards. ''This day and time we have to take extraordinary precautions. It's a dangerous business.''

''I want to trust you, Brandon,'' Max said in all honesty. ''But I know you're not telling me everything. A good liar you're not.''

Brandon exhaled wearily and looked away. ''Yes, there's more.'' His gaze leveled on Max's then. ''We are responsible for Harold Atkins's death. It was my men that Miss Jackson saw. But we did it to protect her. Harold was a spy for Biogenisis. He was selling us out.'' He glanced at the woman behind the tinted glass in the SUV. ''Selling her out and she didn't even know it. When we tried to stop him…'' He shrugged. ''Well, things went wrong.''

''And you're sure,'' Max pressed, ''that Harold Atkins is dead. Who identified the body?''

Brandon looked nervous. ''I…I did. It wasn't easy to tell, with the condition his face was in.'' He sighed, remembering. ''Even with a bullet in his chest, he managed to shoot and kill one of my men. The shots that finished him off were head shots, making ID difficult. But it was him. Though I wasn't there when it happened, I know it was. Just in case, however, we verified his identity with fingerprints.'' He moved his head from side to side. ''I can't believe it came to that…but it did. If we hadn't stopped him, Miss Jackson and her baby would be lab rats for Biogenisis at this very moment. We tried to do the right thing. Even gave the bastard a topnotch funeral.'' His gaze leveled on Max's. ''It had to be done. Now, I'd like to speak to Miss Jackson.''

The door opened and Nicole climbed out of the vehicle, removing the black wig as she emerged.

A gasp sounded from Brandon. "That's...where is she?" He turned and glowered at Max. "Where the hell is she? I'm telling you that Biogenisis is after her. They could have her right now!"

"Now it's your turn to trust me," Max countered. "Miss Jackson is safe. Once you've provided the proof we requested and a signed contract agreeing to our conditions, she will provide you with a signed contract, as well."

Resigned, Brandon nodded. "All right. All right. Just make sure you keep her and that baby safe."

"You have my word," Max said, concluding their meeting.

THE WAITING WAS DRIVING her crazy. Scout paced back across the length of the room. Why hadn't they heard something by now? It shouldn't be taking this long.

"Relax!" Doug implored. "If anything goes wrong, we'll find out. Max and Ryan know what they're doing."

But the men who were after them were ruthless, capable of anything. She'd seen that firsthand. She didn't bother arguing, however.

Moments later she stopped in midstep and threw her hands up in the air. "I can't stand this. Can't we contact someone and find out what's going on?"

"We'll wait for them to contact us," Doug said reassuringly. "If we called, the timing could be bad and cause all sorts of problems."

She understood that, but she needed to know that everything was okay. When she turned to pace in the opposite direction, a telephone rang. Doug checked his, but it wasn't ringing. The next instant their gazes went to the bar. The cellphone that had been delivered to her at the Colby Agency guest house lay there. It rang again. Max had kept it handy in case her ''uncle'' made contact again.

''I'm not sure you should answer it,'' Doug said, pushing himself up from the couch and crossing to the bar as she did.

''What if it's...Uncle Harold again?'' she said, voicing her uncharacteristic fear. He was dead. Wasn't he? God, she didn't know. ''Or what if it's Alexon and they have Max and Nicole?''

Doug shook his head. ''We would know.''

She arched a skeptical eyebrow. ''Would we?''

Before he could answer the question, she snatched up the phone and punched the receive button. ''Hello.''

''Scout, thank God you're okay.''

Gage.

Why would he be calling? What did it take to get rid of him? He'd lied to Max. Had he lied to her? ''What's up, Gage?''

Doug frowned when he heard the name.

''Alexon is going to kill Max. You have to come right away.''

''What?'' A chunk of ice formed in her belly. This was crazy. But...Alexon was with Max. Her heart started to hammer in her chest. ''Max is—''

''The meeting with Maxwell is just a decoy,'' Gage said urgently. ''They knew you wouldn't really show up there with him so they staged a plan B, so to speak. If you don't come right away, he's going to die. Harold is behind everything. He's the one. He tried to get me to come in on the deal and I refused. I'm on my way there to try and stop him.''

He paused. "Let me help you, Scout," he urged. "We can't let them kill Max. I know he's the father of your child and that there can never be anything between us. I have to do the right thing...we have to help Max. And you can finally bring to justice the man who killed your father."

Shock gripped her. She tried to assimilate everything he said, but all she could think about was Max. If this was a setup... But Harold couldn't be involved. He was dead.

But the M.E.'s file is missing, a little voice argued. *The mortician couldn't really say for sure that it was him.* The call...that voice had been his. She was certain of it.

What if Gage was right? What if Harold was alive? What if he and Alexon were hurting Max right this moment?

She scrubbed a hand over her face and tried to make a decision. "Gage, I don't know. I—"

"Please, Scout, you have to trust me. I know I let you down by not standing up to your uncle and stopping him, but you have to believe me now."

"Wait," she ordered. Turning the phone against her shoulder, she looked straight at Doug and demanded, "Is there any way to find out if everything is as it should be with Max and the others?" Her heart thundered in her chest. She had to be sure.

Doug hesitated.

"I have to know. Now!"

Doug punched in a number on his cellular phone. After a brief pause, he said, "I need a status." He listened, then looked at her. "The meeting went down without a glitch. They're headed back here now. ETA is twenty minutes."

Gage was lying.

A cold hard knot formed in her stomach. She lifted the cellphone back to her ear. "Gage?"

Nothing.

She punched the end button and stared blankly at the phone. Why had he made that call? What was the point? Who was he working for? If he knew about the meeting with Alexon…

The answer hit her with all the force of a kick to her solar plexus.

She quickly punched the menu button and advanced to the call log of the cellular phone she still clutched in her hand. *Length of last call: 65 seconds.*

He was tracing the call.

He knew where she was.

Her gaze shifted to Doug's. "We have to get out of here. Now."

As if reading her mind, he grabbed her by her uninjured arm and rushed to the elevator. "Not a good idea," he said on second thought. "The stairs."

They raced down the fourteen floors, flight after flight. Her lungs felt ready to burst, but she kept going. They had to move quickly or Gage would find them.

But why was he doing this? It didn't make sense.

At the first floor, Doug paused and turned around to face her. "Stay behind me."

They moved down to the basement parking garage level. There was no window in the door to check out what they might find outside. The front entrance would likely be covered. All they could do was make a run for it. She nodded, scarcely able to draw a breath, much less utter a word.

Doug drew his weapon and stepped into the underground garage. An eerie silence hung in the air.

The squeal of tires split the silence.

Doug wheeled to the right, guarding her with his body.

The *tap-tap-tap* of gunfire echoed.

Doug went down.

A bullet grazed Scout's thigh before she could reach for him. She swung her weapon in the direction of the threat.

Too late. Gage held a bead right between her eyes.

SCOUT STRUGGLED THROUGH the blackness. She had to wake up, but it kept pushing her back down.

She forced her eyes open and fought the vertigo as the room spun wildly around her.

Her mouth was dry, and when she swallowed it didn't help.

Where was she?

The memory of the race down the stairs and the gunfire suddenly mushroomed in her mind.

Gage.

Doug had been lying on the ground, blood pooling beneath him....

She tried to move, and cried out when pain knifed through her. She'd been hit in the left thigh. Lifting her head as best she could, she tried to see how badly she was hurt. Just a flesh wound, she remembered fuzzily. Her hands and feet were tied. Blood had soaked through the hastily wrapped bandage on her thigh. Another bout of dizziness made her head swim wildly.

She ordered herself to think, to pay attention to

her surroundings. The room was only dimly lit, so she couldn't make out many details. The surface she lay on was some sort of examining table…like the one at the emergency room. A lab…

Fear rocketed through her. They had her!

Alexon had her. That meant Gage was working for them.

She opened her mouth to scream, but swallowed the sound instead. Her screams would only bring the enemy. She needed to find a way to escape. She couldn't do that if they came.

Tears burned her eyes, but she gritted her teeth and blinked them away. Gage, the bastard, would not win. She would find a way out of here.

Max.

She shuddered.

No, she told herself. Max was okay. He was probably looking for her now. *Please, God, let him have gotten back in time to save Doug.*

Okay, okay, she coached herself silently. *Concentrate. Try to get loose.* She struggled against her bonds, but they were so tight she could barely move. Fear and determination drove her. She would wriggle her hands until she worked free. All she needed was time.

A door on the other side of the room swung open and the sound of footsteps announced that someone had entered the room. She froze, closing her eyes and pretending to be asleep, though her heart hammered so hard she was certain whoever it was would hear it. She tried to make her breathing slow and even, but it didn't work.

''Don't play with me, Scout. I know you're awake.''

Her eyes flew open.

Gage.

Fury exploded anew inside her. For the first time in her life she wanted to kill another human being. She struggled against her restraints, praying for just one minute with her hands around his throat.

"You bastard," she hissed. "Who hired you to do this?"

He laughed. "Why, your dear old uncle, of course."

Uncle Harold?

Her heart shuddered to a near stop. Gage had said Harold had killed her father and tried to sell her out. How could he do that? She'd loved him like a second father! He'd professed to love her....

Gage smiled, a sick, sinister expression. "Oh, I know you don't want to believe it, but trust me, it's quite true. Of course, he did love you. Just as he loved your father. But when anything came between Harold Atkins and money—well, let's just say that money always came out the winner."

"I need to know if he really killed my father." She had to know the answer to that. She'd waited a long time. Whatever happened, she needed to be sure if what Gage had told her about Harold and her father was true.

"He did." Gage gave her another of those sick smiles. "I swear it on my mother's grave."

Bastard. How could someone so inhumane even have a mother? "Did he really blackmail you into keeping quiet?" While she had his attention focused on her face and the conversation, she kept working at the restraints. She had to get her hands free.

"Oh, well now, that was a bit of a lie." Kimble

held his thumb and forefinger about an inch apart. "I actually would have done the job myself, but Harold beat me to it. You see, I was Harold's middleman. I still had the contacts in the Defense Department."

She stilled. Her father had died because of this lowlife piece of scum and his equally lowlife partner...Harold Atkins. She would kill Gage Kimble. Too bad Harold was already dead. Then again, was he? Her gaze narrowed with malice.

"Where is Harold?" she demanded, enraged.

"Another stretch of the truth," Gage said with a shrug. "Harold is dead and buried, just as you thought."

"What about the call?"

"That was easy enough to engineer. I had the tape from your answering machine and several taped calls of my own. I must say that stealing the M.E.'s file certainly added to the credibility of my ruse."

Her answering machine? Confusion furrowed her brow. Her brain seemed to fixate on that one part of his confession. "You broke into my house?"

He nodded, feigning contrition. "That was me. I had your line tapped and your friend had called. I couldn't let you get those messages. The last thing I needed was Maxwell involved. Good thing I did, too. That tape came in handy."

"That doesn't make sense. Alexon hired Max."

Kimble flashed another knowing smile. "Ah, but Alexon did not hire me. You see, Alexon has been telling the truth. They tried to protect you from us...but we're much smarter."

This was too much to handle. Her mind spun with

conflicting scenarios. "But Harold worked for Alexon," she argued.

"He was a spy for us."

"Us?"

"Biogenisis. That's my employer. Usually I stay in the background, but our people got so sloppy—" he glanced at her bandaged arm "—I had to step in and take care of the matter personally. Otherwise you might never have known I was involved. I wanted you to trust me. I was certain after I blew up Harold's house that you'd trust me instead of Maxwell. After all, you thought I'd gotten a call to come just as you did. Not that it matters." He looked at his wristwatch then. "Any minute they'll be here for you." He patted her stomach. "And this little gold mine."

A combination of fear and fury rolled through her, sending adrenaline surging. She would not let them hurt her child.

Gage shook his head and sighed. "If you just hadn't been immune to K-141 this would never have happened. Harold really did hate to do this to you, but money is money, after all. When he discovered that you and Maxwell were immune and that you had conceived while in isolation, he knew the resulting fetus would be worth a fortune. Too bad he didn't live to see his plan to fruition."

A phone rang. "Excuse me," Gage said politely as he pulled the cellular phone from his jacket pocket. "Kimble."

Her left hand was almost free. But Scout needed a weapon. While he was distracted by the call, she looked around the room as best she could. There had to be something....

A tray sat on a table next to her. A hypodermic needle lay on it, along with a couple of other medical instruments. She frowned, trying to figure out why the needle would be there. Then she knew. Gage had drugged her to keep her quiet as he ushered her to his vehicle. She remembered that by the time they'd reached his SUV she could scarcely stand. Then she'd blacked out. When the other Biogenisis people arrived they would likely drug her again to facilitate transferring her to wherever the hell they intended to take her.

Please, she prayed, *let Max find me in time.*

But how could he? He had no idea where Gage had taken her. It was up to her.

As luck would have it, two things happened at once in the next second: her left hand came free from the bindings and Gage ended his phone conversation.

Scout reached out, grabbing the hypodermic needle.

"What the hell are—" Gage reached across her.

She swung her left shoulder upward, putting all her strength into the blow as she stabbed the hypodermic into his chest. Instinctively she pushed the plunger downward, expelling the drug into his system.

Screaming curses, he knocked her hand away.

Her right hand came loose then. She sat up.

He pulled the needle free and threw it across the room.

"You bitch!"

She tried to stop him, but somehow his hands wrapped around her throat. She struggled, but he was stronger. He forced her back down onto the table. She pulled his hair and he swore. The pressure on her throat didn't let up. She couldn't breathe. Flailing desperately, she poked him in the eyes with her fingers. He released her and shielded his face with his hands.

Gasping for breath, Scout reached for the bonds holding her feet. Gage staggered toward her again, tending his eyes with one hand and reaching for his gun with the other.

Fear paralyzed her.

He would kill her now.

The weapon leveled on her chest.

She told herself to move.

She couldn't.

The explosion of a gunshot echoed around her.

Scout's breath caught. She stared down at her chest, expecting to see blood cover her T-shirt.

Gage crumpled to the floor.

"Scout! Are you all right?"

Max.

Thank God.

It was Max.

Suddenly he was holding her in his arms. Someone was untying her feet. She couldn't make sense of all that was going on around her, but she was too happy to see Max to care.

He lifted her in his arms and carried her out of the hideous room, down a long corridor and finally into the night air.

Thank God. Thank God.

She and the baby were safe.

When he paused at his SUV to open the door, she remembered Doug Cooper. "Doug? Is he—"

"He's gonna be okay. We got to him only

minutes after the shooting. He was already dragging himself toward his vehicle and trying to use his cell-phone.''

Scout smiled through her tears. ''Can't keep you Colby guys down,'' she said, her voice quavering.

Max kissed her forehead. ''I'm just glad you're okay. I've never been so afraid in my life.''

Scout drew back to look into his eyes, determined to say the words burgeoning in her heart. But pain knifed through her belly, cutting off any possibility of speech. She stiffened, then grabbed her middle. The next stab of pain had her crying out in agony.

''What's wrong?''

''Get me to a hospital, Max.'' Another jolt of agony rendered her mute once more.

The baby.

Something was wrong.

MAX RETRACED HIS STEPS across the waiting room floor. They should have heard something by now. What was going on back there?

Braxton came into the waiting room carrying two cups of steaming coffee. ''Here.'' He offered one to Max. ''Drink this or I may have to shoot you to put you out of your misery.''

Too worried to think about drinking coffee, he took the cup anyway, just to get Braxton off his back. Braxton seemed to have a lot of experience with waiting. He was too damned patient. Max was losing his mind.

''I checked on Cooper,'' Braxton commented as he took a seat. ''He's fine. They'll be moving him from ICU to a private room later tonight.''

''Thank God.'' At least they'd gotten some good

news. Max dropped into the closest chair and tried to force himself to drink the coffee, but his stomach rebelled at the first taste. He suddenly felt the same queasiness he'd suffered the other morning. If he didn't know better, he'd swear he was the one with morning sickness.

"It's a good thing we put our own tracking device in that locket." Braxton waited until Max looked at him. "That was a good call."

Max shrugged. "I was afraid she'd try to give me the slip again. Especially when she heard our plan." He blew out a breath. The waiting was killing him. The gunshot wound to her thigh was superficial, but the sudden onset of abdominal cramping was another story.

"You should speak to Victoria about taking some time off," Braxton counseled. "You and Scout have some things to work out."

He nodded. "You're right about that."

What if she lost the baby? He closed his eyes and fought the burn of emotion in his eyes. *His baby.* He hadn't done enough to keep them safe. Doug had told them how Kimble had tracked her location via the call on the cellular phone. Crafty bastard. Max's only regret was that he hadn't been looking him in the eye when that shot ended his time on this earth.

"Drink up, Max," Braxton encouraged. "I have a feeling you're going to need your strength."

Before Max could respond a nurse stepped into the small waiting room. "Mr. Maxwell?"

Max handed the cup of coffee back to Braxton and stood. "Yes."

"Come with me, please."

Max followed her down a long white corridor. His

gut clenched as the medicinal smell hit him all over again. Finally the nurse paused at one of the treatment room doors. "Go on in. The doctor's waiting for you."

When Max entered the room, he feared the worst. What he found was Scout lying on a table, her still-flat abdomen exposed and a wide smile on her face. The doctor was smoothing a small handheld device over her belly.

"Max!" Those gray eyes beamed at him. Her smile was so contagious he couldn't help smiling back. "Look, it's our baby."

Startled by her words, he moved nearer. She grabbed his hand and pulled him even closer. "Look at the screen."

He studied the screen and then realized what it was. A sonogram.

"See?" Scout urged, excitement in her voice.

Emotion grabbed Max by the heart and wouldn't let go. He could see the baby on the screen. Just a fuzzy outline...but a baby. His baby. Something shifted in his chest and he felt suddenly lightheaded.

"Everything looks just fine, Miss Jackson," the doctor said. "Just a little scare from all the physical and emotional stress, I think. Now that we've got everything calmed down, all looks well. But we'd like to keep you overnight just to be sure."

"Okay." Her fingers tightened around Max's. "Isn't he something?"

Max looked from the screen to her and back. "Or she?" His heart was racing. He was going to be a father.

"Or she," Scout agreed.

"I'll have the nurse print some of these images

for you to keep.'' The doctor smiled as he moved away from the table. ''Just relax for a few moments while I see that you get moved to a private room.''

When the doctor had gone, Max finally tore his gaze away from the image frozen on the screen. ''They're sure everything's okay?''

She nodded. ''Staying the night is just a precaution. I'm fine. They tested my blood for the sedative Gage used. The doctor said the baby wouldn't be hurt by it.''

Just the mention of the son of a bitch's name made Max stiffen with fury. ''Good.''

''Max, I'm sorry I didn't tell you sooner.'' She stared at the image on the screen. ''I had no right to keep this from you.''

He leaned down and kissed her on the forehead. He was so damn thankful she and the baby were safe. ''It's okay. We've both made mistakes.''

She looked at him then, those gray eyes full of uncertainty. ''What do we do now?''

''Biogenisis's activities will be frozen pending a full federal investigation, so I don't think we have anything to worry about there. Alexon has agreed to our terms. I'd say it's safe to assume you can have your life back now.''

She nodded. ''That's wonderful.'' She moistened those sweet lips and looked up at him, a vulnerability in her eyes he'd never seen before. ''But what about us?''

He smiled then, his heart ready to burst with emotion. ''I'd say we have a lot of plans to make.'' He shrugged. ''You know, a wedding, a bigger house.'' It was his turn to feel uncertain then. ''That is, if that's what you want. I hadn't thought about your business down in Houston.''

She nibbled that lower lip, making him yearn to do the same. ''I was thinking that I might just turn the business over to Donna and join the Colby Agency. That is,'' she qualified, echoing his words, ''if they can use another good agent.''

''I think I can guarantee that,'' Max assured her, then winked. ''I have an inside track with the boss.''

A smile bloomed on those lush lips. ''But what if we can't get along? I mean, we both like being in charge. Who's going to be the boss?''

Max kissed the hand holding his and then kissed those tempting lips. ''How about we take turns?''

She kissed him back, a slow, lingering kiss.

When at last they came up for air, she countered, ''Only if I can be the boss first.''

''Anything you want, sweetheart. Anything you want.''

''Deal,'' she murmured as his mouth claimed hers once more to seal the bargain that would last a lifetime.

Epilogue

Doug Cooper sat in Victoria Colby's office, anticipation mounting inside him. He'd been stuck on desk duty since taking that bullet six weeks ago. Lucky for him it hadn't hit anything vital, just put him out of commission temporarily.

But now he was ready to get back to work. Victoria had assured him that she would be assigning him lead on his first case very soon, and that had been before the shooting. He hoped the meeting this morning would be to brief him on a new assignment—one in which he would act as lead investigator. He was more than ready.

Scout Jackson—Scout Maxwell, he amended—was doing great, as well. Thankfully, one of Alexon's top scientists had discovered that a plant both Scout and Max had been exposed to long-term while living in Colombia had stimulated their immunity to K-141. With that knowledge, scientists could use the plant to create the antidote, eliminating the need to involve Scout or her child any further. Doug, as well as everyone at the Colby Agency, was immensely relieved. That nightmare was finally over.

"I apologize for keeping you waiting, Douglas,"

Victoria said as she breezed in, looking as elegant as ever. She settled behind her wide mahogany desk and smiled. "You look fit and ready to get back into the field."

He nodded. "I am. I'd like to start immediately."

She studied him a moment. "I've put a great deal of thought into who I would assign to this rather sensitive case, and I really do feel that you would be the right man for the job."

A smile stretched across Doug's face. "Thank you, Victoria. I can assure you that I won't let you down."

"Don't thank me yet, Douglas. You haven't heard the assignment."

Uneasiness slid through him.

"I know that you prefer to keep your background out of your life these days."

The uneasiness turned to wariness. "That's correct."

"But this case demands someone with a polished, high-society background, I'm afraid. Unfortunately, Simon isn't available, since he's taken over Max's caseload while he honeymoons with his wife. That leaves only you."

Doug almost said no without even hearing the details, but the desire to make this next move up the ladder kept him silent. "What does the case involve?"

"Solange D'Martine was thought to be the final surviving heir to the D'Martine jewelry empire, an American-based company with international connections."

Doug knew the family name. If memory served him correctly, the D'Martines were of Martha's

Vineyard, just as his family was. "I'm familiar with the name," he said dryly.

"Well, it seems that Solange D'Martine's son, who was kidnapped and murdered some twenty years ago, left behind an heir whose existence wasn't known about until recently."

Doug knew a little about the case. The son had been the sole heir to the empire, which had its roots in France. The son had been held for ransom and something had gone terribly wrong. His father had died shortly after the horrific event from a heart attack, brought on, most believed, by the tragedy.

"As you can well imagine, this would be a very high-profile case."

Doug nodded, more certain now than ever that he wanted no part of it.

"The heir, a young woman, needs a personal bodyguard while the technical issues are resolved. Mrs. D'Martine fears that if the media got wind of her existence, her safety would be in question. After what happened to the son, I can understand her feelings. She would like the young woman watched twenty-four-seven until she is ready to go public with the announcement."

Doug raised a skeptical eyebrow. "And when would that be? After DNA has proved the heir legitimate?"

Victoria shook her head. "They've already established that issue."

"What's the holdup then?"

"The young woman is unaware of her heritage."

Doug sat up straighter. "No one has spoken to her?" He shook his head. "I don't even want to know how they managed to establish paternity."

"Suffice to say that money can buy just about anything," Victoria commented sagely.

A truer statement had never been spoken. Doug knew firsthand. "So what does Mrs. D'Martine expect me to do?"

"You are to approach the young woman along with the family attorney. He will relay the details and you're to stay behind when he leaves."

"Let me get this straight." Doug almost laughed. "Once the attorney tells her that her whole life is a lie—that whoever she believes her father is…isn't—I'm supposed to keep her company until they iron out all the issues?"

"Precisely."

Doug didn't miss the twinkle of amusement in Victoria's eyes. "This heiress," Doug ventured. "What exactly is her life like now?"

"Quite sedate, I'm told. She's a plumber in a small town in Maryland."

Startled, Doug could only manage a strained laugh. "A plumber?"

Victoria nodded. "This is why I need you for this assignment, Doug. You of all people understand what this young woman is about to go through. She needs the kind of help only you can give."

Doug got it then. He might be a little slow on the uptake, but he was there now. "I see," he said knowingly. "The whole bodyguard thing is really just a sham—"

Victoria lifted a hand, cutting him off. "The security concern is real," she insisted. "There is always a risk when this kind of wealth is involved. That the son was kidnapped and murdered and the case remains unsolved only increases the risk."

Doug refused to relent. "Still, the bottom line is that while the 'technicalities' are being worked out, you want me to turn this plumber into a princess."

Victoria gave a succinct nod. "Precisely."

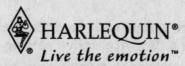

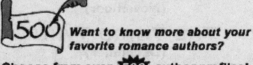

An offer you can't afford to refuse!

High-valued coupons for upcoming books

**A sneak peek at Harlequin's newest line—
Harlequin Flipside™**

**Send away for a hardcover by *New York Times*
bestselling author Debbie Macomber**

How can you get all this?

Buy four Harlequin or Silhouette books during
October–December 2003, fill out the form below and send
the form and four proofs of purchase (cash register receipts)
to the address below.

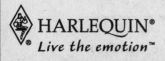

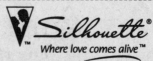

Visit us at www.eHarlequin.com

Q42003

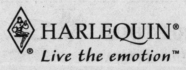

HARLEQUIN®
INTRIGUE®

has a new lineup of books to keep you on the edge of your seat throughout the winter. So be on the alert for...

BACHELORS AT LARGE

Bold and brash—these men have sworn to serve and protect as officers of the law...and only the most special women can "catch" these good guys!

UNDER HIS PROTECTION
BY AMY J. FETZER
(October 2003)

UNMARKED MAN
BY DARLENE SCALERA
(November 2003)

BOYS IN BLUE
A special 3-in-1 volume with
REBECCA YORK (Ruth Glick writing as Rebecca York),
ANN VOSS PETERSON AND PATRICIA ROSEMOOR
(December 2003)

CONCEALED WEAPON
BY SUSAN PETERSON
(January 2004)

GUARDIAN OF HER HEART
BY LINDA O. JOHNSTON
(February 2004)

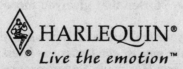

HARLEQUIN®
Live the emotion™

**Visit us at www.eHarlequin.com
and www.tryintrigue.com**

HIBBONTS

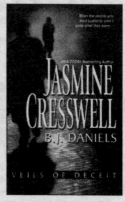